A ROTTEN BUSINESS

SIMON HARE

*Oh what a tangled web we weave
when first we practise to deceive*

Sir Walter Scott

*But when we've practised for a while
How vastly we improve our style*

A.R.Pope

Notes from the Author

A Rotten Business is a satirical work of fiction. Thankfully, Sprayum and Scarper does not exist and neither do any of its employees. Any resemblance to any persons living, moribund or dead is coincidental. It would of course be most reassuring to confirm that this statement also includes the Reginald Grimshaw's of this world. Unfortunately this might be wishful thinking.

Chapter One

I remember it all started one grey drizzly November morning back in 1982.

The letter I received from my friendly bank manager Mr Grimshaw certainly came as a complete surprise. In it he kept talking about 'reducing his exposure'.

In the years I had known him I had certainly never witnessed him exposing himself and I really couldn't understand why he felt the need to make this confession to me. I had always imagined him to be an upright stable and happily married fellow; a highly respected pillar of the establishment and certainly not a perverted sexual deviant. Assuming that he was suffering from some sort of mental breakdown I thought it advisable to ignore the letter and carry on working. But then a couple of weeks later a second letter arrived explaining that he was now feeling extremely vulnerable and couldn't risk exposing himself any longer. This was quickly followed up with a statutory demand giving me seven days to live; something about execution or perhaps it was executing proceedings, I can't exactly remember. What transpired after that was indeed quite farcical but I shall return to that later. There certainly wasn't much work around at this time; a direct result I fear, of too many bank managers exposing themselves. Jobs in the building trade particularly for carpenters were virtually non existent. When I realised what was happening my thoughts at the time alternated between suicide and perhaps a life of crime.

For the past fifteen years I had been running my own small but nonetheless profitable building company.

The recession of the last two years was still biting hard; the ramifications of it were noticeable everywhere, but as is normally the case the building and allied trades were the first to suffer. Once the paranoia started a general squeeze by the banks and a ruthless turning of the screw as far as their revised lending criteria was concerned forced many small businesses into liquidation and bankruptcy. I had always had a fairly optimistic outlook in respect of my own business; a good deal of the work I did was for medium to large sized property companies whom I had known for many years and always paid up on time.

Unfortunately, the two clients owing me the most, both went to the wall at the same time. In view of this my own position suddenly looked slightly precarious. The prospect now of having to abandon everything I had worked for including the few loyal employees that had stood by me through thick and thin was totally abhorrent. Even more unpalatable was the ignominious outcome of having to 'get a job'. After fifteen years of self employment I had undoubtedly become arrogant. Generally speaking I was the person making the decisions; I chose which jobs I would take on, I priced them, I employed the other trades I needed and I paid the wages and the bills. Somehow I would have to recover a few shreds of humility. I knew this wasn't going to be at all easy. Looking through my local newspaper I came across a large advertisement;

'Trainee House Inspectors required for a Woodworm and Damp Proofing Company. Presentable people with some building experience required for our Brighton branch. High earning potential. Applicants must be willing to undergo a six week training course at our head office in Southampton.'

I had always been deeply suspicious of these companies; particularly the activities and sales methods employed by their 'inspectors' or surveyors as they are sometimes fancifully described. However, this was no time to pick and choose I needed to eat and pay the mortgage. Various loans to the bank were secured against the house I lived in but I would have to worry about that later as the noose was tightened. I picked up the phone and dialled the number in the advert.

"Good morning, Sprayum and Scarper, Jill speaking how may I help you?"

"I've erm . . . called about the advert . . . for home inspectors."

"Ah yes, would you like to come in for an interview?" Jill replied in a happy sing song voice.

"I think so," I said reluctantly, "although I would like to know a little more about the job. Can you give me anymore details?"

"No I'm afraid not," the voice sang out, "you will need to see our Mr Martin. I can offer you three o'clock this afternoon, or eleven or twelve thirty tomorrow."

"Eleven tomorrow would be a good time for me," I replied, desperately trying to sound enthusiastic.

After singing the directions out Jill told me to 'have a nice day, and put the phone down.

I certainly didn't have a nice day. I had acquired a number of strange symptoms: headaches, nausea, a weird looking skin rash on my arms and legs and most worrying of all; a large painful lump had erupted on my back between my shoulder blades. I tried not to speculate on what sort of terrifying life threatening disease was developing, despite my doctor's diagnoses that stress was probably at the heart of it. Stress after all was as good a guess as any. The prospect now of becoming a woodworm inspector was after all stressful beyond any human comprehension; particularly for me. The rest of the day was spent telephoning clients and explaining that I would be unable to complete their half finished building projects.

Several times I managed to resist the overwhelming compulsion to phone Sprayum and Scarper and explain that since I last spoke to them half an hour ago; I had just received a telephone call from my doctor telling me that I'd only got a few weeks to live and cancel the appointment. There were many nagging doubts about the supposed wisdom of subjecting myself to any further degrading humiliation but I knew something had to be done.

Tim Martin, or 'TM' as he preferred to be called; was a large fellow probably in his fifty's. He must have been about six foot three, large boned and somewhat menacing in appearance. The skin around his face was pot marked and sallow. His enormous nose was a distinctly different colour to the rest of his face and resembled a large gnarled turnip. What little grey hair there was on the sides of his cadaverous head was trained neatly over his ears almost half covering them. The remainder of his head glistened under the fluorescent light above his desk; it appeared to be covered in a film of light machine oil. The penetrating light grey eyes sited under his heavy eyelids reminded me of an SS commandant in a P.O.W camp; the sort of person that always used to appear in sixties and seventies war films in that amateurish form of Technicolor. Despite the expensive ill fitting blue suit that hung about his bulk I now knew who he was, I also knew now where I was. This was actually a prison camp and he was in charge of it. Well at least we know where we are now. I did think there was something strange about this place as soon as I walked in.

"You don't sound much like a builder to me if you don't mind me saying so," he said almost accusingly. "Your accent...sounds more like...well, like someone that's had a decent education."

"Well, I did other things before I got involved in the building trade," I replied.

"Really? What things?"

"It's a long story," I started to explain; "when I left school I did a carpentry apprenticeship; which allowed me to become the world's leading authority on sweeping up wood shavings: I then spent a few years working for an estate agent whilst studying to become a chartered surveyor. I then concluded that they were a fairly objectionable breed and decided to try something different."

"Which of them did you find 'objectionable'?" he enquired, "was it the estate agents or the chartered surveyors?"

"Oh both of them," I replied without a seconds hesitation. "I then studied for a degree in economics and became a credit analyst for a large credit card company. I quickly became very disillusioned with this and at twenty five I started my own small building company."

"Well it takes all sorts," he said. I wasn't exactly sure what this was supposed to infer but just nodded politely. I detected from the cautious look in his eyes that he was probably wondering which secure psychiatric unit I had just escaped from and whether I might in fact be dangerous.

Then after what clearly came across as smug commiserations about my unfortunate circumstances and my bank managers desire to restrict his indecent exposure; we got straight down to business.

"What do you know about woodworm?" he asked.

"Well... they eat wood I guess and leave little holes in it."

"Anything else?"

"Well, yes; if there are enough of them and the problem isn't sorted out they can cause a certain amount of structural damage I suppose."

"That's it, that's precisely it," he said excitedly, "this is the problem. The beetles lay eggs you see; normally in the region of sixty to eighty of them at a time. These eggs hatch into larvae which bore their way into the timber and chew away at it to their hearts content for anything up to five years;

9

they then emerge as adult beetles, lay more eggs and the cycle is repeated."

"Quite a boring life for them really," I said with a foolish attempt at humour.

"It's not a joke," he said sternly. "Woodworm causes millions of pounds worth of damage to properties every year. Our task here is to find them, and eradicate them before they completely destroy people's houses."

"Yes, I do understand," I said, bitterly regretting my flippant remark.

"Your job here; if we decide to employ you; will be to carry out inspections of properties and then prepare estimates for eradicating the woodworm. You will inspect roof spaces, floors and basically any timbers that you can gain access to; whenever you come across any evidence of it you quote to treat it; are you with me?"

"Yes, of course, by evidence presumably you mean the eggs and the holes they leave in the timber?"

"No, no, no, not the eggs: the eggs are microscopic; you'd never be able to see their eggs with the naked eye. You look for the holes . . . they're called flight holes or exit holes, where the adult beetle has just emerged. Do you understand what I'm talking about?" he said getting redder and redder.

"Yes I do, I understand exactly," I said, fearing that he was about to spontaneously combust.

"Where these holes are there will be little piles of bore dust which is called 'frass'. The holes themselves will be fresh bore holes with sharp crisp edges to them; they're very easy to see; in fact you can't miss them."

There was however, one question I had to ask but didn't want to appear stupid. It seemed to me that if you can't see the eggs; and there are no flight holes; there would be no reason to suppose that a problem exists; when there must be instances where the timbers look perfectly sound but were really full of larvae who had now developed into fine upstanding members of the beetle community and were contemplating their imminent emergence. If this were the case, then some timbers that might have been decreed 'sound, could a short time later, be peppered with flight holes thereby transforming what was hitherto a perfect structure into a perforated husk. Throwing caution to the wind I decided to pose this very proposition.

"Excellent, good, good, I pleased you've thought about that. This is exactly the problem we are faced with," he said, looking quite animated. "You can never be to sure. The best thing to do is always err on the side of caution. We have a little saying here which is: 'the only way to beat 'em' is to treat 'em'."

"Right, so does this mean that if 'they' are there, we quote to treat them; but if 'they' are not there we still quote to treat them anyway just in case they could be there?"

"Yup, you've got in one."

Although it was taking some time I was beginning to understand the difficult dilemma we were facing. However, I felt a few points needed further clarification. The first question I asked seemed to fire his enthusiasm so what the hell, I decided to continue;

"So let me get this right," I said, now returning the fixed humourless stare which I gathered was a prerequisite when discussing the boring habits of woodworm. "I go around to peoples houses and look for woodworm. I will know its there because of the bore dust and flight holes they make when exiting the timber; if I see evidence of this then presumably I draw their attention to it?"

"That's exactly right," he confirmed, looking a little puzzled.

"If there is no evidence how do I convince them that the timbers should be treated anyway?"

"No, no, that's actually a good question," he said nodding vigorously.

"You'll be doing these inspections with one of our fully trained and qualified house inspectors so don't worry too much about that at the moment. Basically, if you can't find just one flight hole or some bore dust anywhere then you must say so. This, as you can appreciate, could be a legal issue attracting all the 'do gooders' on the planet from trade descriptions to consumer protection, the pope, the bishop and Christ knows who else. What you say when you submit your report to the customer, is that 'at the time of our inspection we were unable to find any positive evidence of the insect'."

"But we think it still could be hiding or hanging around in there somewhere?" I interrupted.

"Yes, but you don't say you think they're hiding somewhere; that's not going to sound very professional. What you do is then insert a little paragraph which is on the word processor, explaining a few basic facts about the problems this insect can cause and the damage it can do before any visual signs are noticed. The paragraph ends with a line saying 'we then, strongly recommend precautionary treatment'. This usually sows the seeds of doubt and secures the contract."

"That's amazing," I said without thinking. "Are people really convinced by this?"

"Well, yes, most people are but if they are not then it's your job to convince them. Right, do you have any more questions?"

"Erm, no, not at this stage." I could sense that he was now becoming a little irritated by my obvious scepticism.

TM then hauled himself up from the large swivel chair behind his desk and proffered a hand for me to shake which resembled a gigantic bunch of swollen bananas.

"We also deal with rot in timber: you know, wet rot, dry rot all that sort of thing as well as wall ties and cavity wall insulation. As I say if we decide to employ you you'll be under the wing so to speak, of one of our experienced home inspectors for the first six weeks which you will spend here on our training programme. After that you will be working at our Brighton office and you will be on your own. At the moment we've got a manager there, and another inspector. In confidence I can tell you that we're not happy with either of them. It seems they would both prefer to sit on their backsides rather than go out and sell the treatments. There are four operatives working there at present and as far as we can tell only one of them is worth his salt; so there's going to be some major changes all round. A general shake up if you understand my meaning. The prospects for you with us are good provided of course that you are able to grasp the basic essentials of the business. I must point out to you though we are not looking for 'boffins'. Once you have qualified your position with us here will have a dual role. You will be required to identify various problems people have and most important are likely to have with their properties and at the same time sell them the appropriate remedial treatment. It's no bloody good to us if you happen to be an expert on the problems if you can't sell the solutions. We're not a charitable advisory body. Do I make myself clear?" he said, shouting almost threateningly.

"Absolutely, I'd very much like to give it a try," I replied, trying even more desperately to sound sincere and enthusiastic.

A few days later I heard that one of my clients a property developer, feeling that he had been treated rather unfairly by his bank asphyxiated himself in his garage by connecting a hose from the exhaust pipe into his car. That scuppers any chances of any 'come backs' for him I thought. Perhaps I should have shown him the advert from Sprayum & Scarper.

Strangely enough, that very morning, a letter arrived from Sprayum & Scarper which was buried amongst the assortment of bills and final demands that were now appearing on a regular basis. The letter signed by TM stated that they were prepared to offer me the position of trainee house inspector on the strict understanding that if I failed to pass the exam they were to set after six weeks training I would be dismissed immediately. If I passed this but failed to meet the company's monthly sales targets, I would on the first transgression have to attend a disciplinary hearing after which the usual punishment would be one hundred lashes. Any further failures could result in the amputation of an ear. Should I still them be unable to achieve the minimum sales required; electrodes to the genitals could not be ruled out. So basically everything looked quite promising.

The following Monday morning I arrived as instructed at the grim soulless looking premises of Sprayum & Scarper still intrigued to some extent to see how things would develop. A number of poor unfortunates apart from myself were stamping around outside in the early morning frost. I was told that they were waiting for Soakum to arrive who was the office manager. A few moments later, a bearded dissipated figure with very bloodshot eyes appeared with the keys. 'Soakum's a lovely man,' one of the women whispered in my ear, 'only he's got a bit of a drink problem if you know what I mean'.

After uttering a string of expletives, something to do with the cold and the traffic, Soakum unlocked the massive peeling wooden doors that led through a sort of workshop area to some narrow stairs which led up to the offices. A number of vans were now drawing up outside the premises. They were all very professionally sign written with 'Sprayum & Scarper, Woodworm, Dry Rot, Rising Damp. Under this was a caption saying 'The Company You Can Trust'.

Once inside the building, I sensed the same aura of tension that I had noticed at the interview. A sort of underlying fear and trepidation. The members of staff that had now arrived were hurriedly taking up their positions. There was noticeably very little small talk or conversation. Any conversation that did take place seemed deadly serious and was in frightened whispers. Soakum, introduced himself, breathed some pretty potent alcohol fumes over me and told me to follow him across the building to the 'inspector's room'. This was a long narrow room with a number of old wooden desks placed in two rows from front to back, which reminded me of an early Victorian school classroom. The first thing I noticed was the vile fetid odour that hit me as he opened the door: stale chip fat, sweat and cigarette smoke. There were several dirty threadbare rugs on the timber floor. In one corner opposite the entrance door was a portable gas heater fizzing away like an angry beast. The condensation caused by this was streaming down the rusted metal window frames and onto the floor. At the back of the room furtively huddled in a corner were the inspectors. There were four of them all wearing voluminous blue nylon overalls and clutching clipboards and sheaths of papers. As I advanced towards them I heard one of them say 'right Stitchum, E's yours'. Stitchum was thirty two years old but looked much younger. He was about five feet ten inches and slightly chubby. He had a permanent vacant expressionless almost moronic face with eyes set close together. He seemed to have little interest or perception of what was going on in the outside world. His life as far as I could tell revolved around 'inspections', complying with the unending list of rules and regulations set down by his employers and of course, most critically meeting the minimum monthly sales targets. Trying to discuss something with him that he didn't quite understand or wasn't directly interested in which of course covered a wide spectrum initiated a series of involuntary body movements starting with the head and neck that quickly affected the shoulders and upper torso. As this developed and his boredom threshold was quickly reached he would say 'right let us not stray from the particular subject matter in question'. He'd had a few odd jobs after leaving school and at nineteen joined the police force where he'd remained until two years ago when he joined Sprayum & Scarper. He was not really that unintelligent more unimaginative and exceedingly boring and mundane. All of this would have been much easier to accept if he had of been blessed with a sense of humour. Whether he did ever have one or whether his time

15

in the police force destroyed it I wouldn't hazard a guess. I suppose it was quite possible that the rigid Machiavellian doctrine together with the pressure of achieving his monthly sales figures at Sprayum & Scarper finally destroyed whatever flimsy vestiges there were. The strange thing about him was the way he spoke and formed sentences. Virtually every statement he made had the 'ring' of a policeman about it. What was even more extraordinary was that the 'clients' and customers he approached seemed somehow beguiled and won over by this tiresome monotone.

"Come in mate," he shouted, as I walked towards this furtive nylon coated group.

"My name's Stitchum, you must be Clive, right?"

"Yeah, that's right," I confirmed, "pleased to meet you."

"TM mentioned that you would be starting today. You're going to be with me for the first couple of weeks so let's hope we get on," he said ominously.

"Can't see any reason why we wouldn't," I said, which was a complete lie. I could already see a million reasons.

The other three inspectors nodded cautiously at me. Stitchum proceeded to introduce them. Robbum was a mean weasel faced man of about fifty, quite short and frail looking. Trickum was a shifty looking villain of about forty with a Mexican moustache with what appeared to be some egg yolk attached to the left hand side of it; and Cheatum, who was without doubt one of the most unsavoury looking characters I have ever seen. Evidently he was an ex car salesman, an ex double glazing salesman and now a house inspector. He was about thirty five years old had a general unwashed greasy appearance with longish black hair heavily gelled and combed back over his head. His fingernails were long and black; the nicotine stained fingers of each hand sported a number of badly scratched and dented gold sovereign rings.

"Watch yer back here mate," he advised me. "They don't take prisoners, no wot I mean?"

"Yeah, I think I do," I said, I was really wondering how it was that this particular fellow was able to convince people of anything at al, but particularly to part with their money.

"Now, we've got four inspections to do this morning Stitchum explained, so we can't stand around here all day. Before we start though I'll take you around the building here quickly and explain how it all works. This room we're in now is what you might call the operations centre. This area is strictly for us the inspectors. We go out in the morning or early afternoon, do the inspections and then come back here to phone the customers, confirm any bookings and most important of all sell the deals. You know…persuade the people who may not have been at the properties we have visited that they need to have the work done; and more importantly: done by us. There are fourteen operatives that do the work in pairs. That means every day seven vans leave here and go off in all directions. The pressure is on us to make sure that they are never standing around here idle with the guv'nors having to pay them. Whenever that happens which it does occasionally you'll wish you'd never been born. Believe me. The guv'nors come in here walk up and down and tell you how much it's costing them. Anyway, that's not been a problem for a while so follow me and I'll show you the work planning room and how that works."

This was along a long dark narrow corridor and was a brightly lighted room with a massive white board extending one metre from the floor up to the ceiling almost covering one wall. The board was ruled off into squares with the days of the month running along the top and the names of the various teams of operatives running down the side. Soakum, was in charge of this operation and was assisted by two receptionists who were seated either side of the board. As we entered the room Soakum was swaying around precariously on a pair of steps writing the addresses of various properties in the boxes. Both women were busy staring at this board whilst talking to customers and booking in 'treatments' on the telephone. The

17

whole thing reminded me of a war planning room. It certainly was a well oiled machine running like clockwork. Next to this room was the typing pool; a hive of industry with four young girls tapping away on large primitive looking word processors. The walls around the four tables where they were seated were shelved from floor to ceiling; each shelf housed piles of printed paraphernalia that accompanied each report and estimate. I was now becoming even more curious to see and understand how this operation worked. Next to this area was a large kitchen, the walls of which were covered with red warning notices. Most of these were in respect of cleanliness and hygiene and were certainly not of a subtle nature. The male and female toilets adjoined the kitchen and again the walls of these were adorned with warnings and threatening notices which seemed to cover everything from sexually transmitted diseases to a list of punishments that would be imposed if anyone was caught spending more than the suggested time allowed for certain bodily functions. Opposite the toilets were the directors 'suites'. There were two directors; Tim Martin, and evidently a much younger man called Andrew Stone who as yet, I had not met.

"TM is hard but fair," Stitchum said quietly. "Andrew is psychopathic nutter. He can seem pleasant one minute and then in a flash without any apparent provocation he flies into an uncontrollable violent rage. About three weeks ago he punched an operative in the face because the customer complained that there were black marks on the walls around the loft hatch where this poor sod had just sprayed the roof timbers. My advice to you is to try and keep out of his way. If you make a mistake or do something wrong for example: if a job goes 'bent' it might be that you have under estimated the amount of chemical required or have missed something you should have picked up on the initial inspection; some rotten timbers or floorboards for example: if you can't get any extra money from the customer and they start talking about complaining and you know the firm's going to lose money on the job; the first thing to do is go and see Soakum; it might be that there's some bits of timber left over from another job that he can lose without anyone finding out. If he can't help and he normally does, particularly if you happen to mention a bottle of scotch; then make sure Andrew's not around and go and see TM."

"How is he likely to react to this sort of thing?"

"Well, as I said he's hard but fair. The last time it happened on one of my jobs was when I missed some rotten floorboards. The owner of the house was what is known in polite circles as a complete arsehole. He wasn't just going to complain to the firm, he was threatening to contact trade descriptions, his solicitor and the local newspapers. I decided the only thing to do was to tell TM and make a clean breast of it so to speak."

"What happened?" I asked, desperate to hear the rest of this.

"Well he was very understanding. He said I would be let off with a written warning provided I paid for the extra costs of the job. I didn't have to pay it in one go. It was deducted out of my wages over a three month period. He really is a very fair man. If that had of been Andrew I probably would have ended up in hospital."

"Yes, I see what you mean; a very magnanimous gesture."

"To be quite honest though, I've been thinking seriously about going back in the force."

"What, you mean the police force?"

"Yeah, I left two years ago because the wife and I were struggling a bit; you know big mortgage, two young kids and it was difficult. There's no doubt you can earn more money in this game but the pressure's been affecting my nerves. I had to see the doctor a few months ago because I was suffering from panic attacks and couldn't get an erection."

"What do you mean? Did you normally get an erection with a panic attack?"

19

"Of course not they were separate problems. When it got near to the end of the month I used to lie awake at night wondering if I would meet the minimum sales target. I knew that if I didn't there would be a disciplinary meeting which would be followed up by the first warning letter. If you have to attend a second hearing within three months of the first you get a second letter and basically one more chance. If you fail to meet the target within the next three months you are given one last chance. Any failures after that don't warrant discussion. You will quite simply be out on your ear. Basically it's all stress, pressure and no security. The rules and regulations here are never ending. It's bad enough in the police force but compared to being here its child's play. A few weeks ago I was laid up with flu: I'd been off for three days and felt like shit. On the fourth day at eight o'clock in the morning Andrew phoned and asked me how I was. I thought it was pretty decent of him to be concerned. 'Feeling pretty awful at the moment', I said. He then asked me if I was worried about achieving my minimum sales target for the month. 'Not at the moment', I said, 'I feel to rough to think about it'. 'Well you should be worried', he said, 'so far your sales for the month are only nine thousand pounds and there are only another five days left for you to get to the minimum'. The next day I came in, dying on my feet I was but managed to pull in twelve local authority houses. All of the roof spaces needing spraying for woodworm which just got me off the hook at the eleventh hour. I was home and dry, well for that month at least."

"Did they all have woodworm?" I asked innocently.

"Of course not but the local authorities are an easy touch. Whenever they prepare a specification for 'refurbs' or improvements; they always allow a sum for woodworm treatments. Sound thinking as far as we're concerned."

"You mentioned the commission structure; how does this work?"

"Easy really, you get paid a basic wage as a house inspector which is not enough to feed a cat on. The rest of it is commission. You don't get any commission on the first twelve thousand pounds worth of sales each month. This is the minimum you must secure to remain employed. They say this just covers the cost of employing one inspector and a car. Funny, I thought when they told me this: the basic wage is only six grand a year so according to them the old Ford Granada I use is costing a hundred and thirty eight grand a year. I never realized that motoring was so expensive. But, no, I digress, so after the first twelve thousand it's all worked out in percentages. You get two per cent on sales between twelve thousand and eighteen thousand and three per cent on any sales over eighteen thousand up to twenty five thousand. Over twenty five thousand it's five per cent. But only two of us have ever achieved that in the time I've been here."

"Clever thinking really," I said out loud. I was trying to do a quick mental calculation of the annual turnover of this enterprise.

"What are the other problems you were talking about you know, all the rules and regulations?"

"Oh, it's endless mate. If you are five minutes late in the morning although there might be nothing happening they stop an hour's pay no matter what the reason is. If your car happens to be seen outside a cafe between any hours other than one to two p.m. they automatically deduct a full days pay. It might be that you have been closing the sale on the deal of the century and decided to carry on working through your lunch time and then get something to eat. This actually happened to me last year. A middle aged couple had just moved into a bungalow in one of the expensive areas not far from here. On the job sheet it said check floors for woodworm. What had happened is that they had bought the place for cash and didn't bother with a survey. But once they'd moved in a carpet fitter working there told them there was woodworm in the floors. When I arrived the woman was

21

dancing about almost hysterical: the prospect of having 'these things' living under floor and in the timbers obviously completely freaked her. I offered to treat all the floors with our insecticide but she wasn't convinced it would kill them all. I did in fact sympathize with her, so much so that I came up with the perfect solution. Fit new flooring throughout. It took me over two hours to sell the idea to them but in the end I won and walked away with a signed acceptance for over six grand. I missed the one to two o'clock lunch time slot but in view of my success I decided to stop at a fast food restaurant on the way back to the office. It must have been about three o'clock in the afternoon. I was absolutely ravenous, I was sitting there enjoying the delights of a triple cheeseburger when who do you think walked through the bloody door?"

"I've got no idea," I said, waiting eagerly for the rest of the story.

"It was Andrew with his two kids from some marriage or other. It was half term."

"What happened?" I almost shouted, quite desperate now to hear the rest of the story.

"Well, he was standing at the serving area; he turned around, and saw me. He stopped dead in his tracks. He had a manic murderous looking expression on his face. He pointed at me and shouted, 'Oi, you, you're not supposed to be in here'. There were about half a dozen other people in the restaurant and it went deadly silent you could have heard a pin drop. I don't think I have ever been so scared and embarrassed in my life. He then walked very slowly over to the table where I was sitting lent over and whispered 'You've got three minutes, eat your food and go. I want to see you in my office at five o'clock this afternoon'. He then stood up and smiled at the other people in the restaurant as if nothing had happened and sat down with his kids.

"I was shaking like a bloody leaf with both fear and anger I suppose. I couldn't finish the cheeseburger or the coffee. I had this burning, buzzing sort of feeling in my head. I got in the car and drove half way along the road towards the office. I stopped the car to gather my thoughts. I was seriously thinking of turning up at five o'clock and killing him. I kept going over in my mind what I would say to him but nothing or none of the arguments or explanations was remotely satisfactory. I can tell you honestly mate if I didn't have two young kids I would have gone in there and beaten him to a pulp."

"So what happened at five o'clock?"

"Well, when I went in TM was with him; calmed him down a bit I think. I showed them the order form I had managed to get signed for six thousand pounds worth of work which really was or should have been a simple woodworm job worth a few hundred pounds. I also pointed out that working on their price structure the total cost would have been just under four grand. To put it in a nutshell I stuck another couple of grand on the job because I knew they would have it done anyway. I knew that the profit on the job on their price structure anyway was one hundred per cent. I was feeling extremely angry; I had worked through my lunch hour to make them something in the region of four thousand pounds profit which they certainly would not have had if I hadn't of used my wits. In the end TM conceded that under the circumstances I hadn't actually committed a criminal offence by stopping for a cheeseburger despite the fact that it was not during the permitted hours. It was agreed that some degree of mitigation would in this instance be taken into consideration and that no further disciplinary measures or punishments would be implemented. As I was walking out of their office TM said; 'By the way Stitchum, good work, keep it up'.

"To be honest, I think it was those last few pleasant words of encouragement that persuaded me to carry on. I didn't sleep for weeks after that, and I haven't been able to look at a triple cheeseburger since. I was still feeling deep anger, frustration and humiliation. Anyway, enough of this waffle;

we've got to get cracking. We've got four properties to look at today. Pop into see Soakum in the work planning room and he'll give you some overalls. I'll see you outside; my car is on the forecourt."

Chapter Two

I quickly donned the massive blue nylon overall that Soakum produced and was feeling slightly light headed from the fumes of his breath. Outside a strong gust of wind hit me as I was walking towards the car inflating the flimsy overall transforming me into a sort of walking balloon. Just a few minutes later and with more than a considerable degree of trepidation on my part, we were heading towards our first 'inspection'.

This turned out to be a 1950's ex-council house which had just been bought by a young couple with a vast collection of screaming red faced babies. The owner of the house was a young lad of about twelve, he nervously handed Stitchum a copy of his mortgage offer.

"It says on here that we must have a timber and damp survey carried out within six months of completion," he said, looking rather like a child that was about to be scolded for being naughty. "We've been here five months, so I thought we must get it sorted out in case there's a problem with the building society."

"Quite right," Stitchum confirmed. "You don't want any problems with them do you? We'll start in the roof and then work our way down through the house."

We crawled about in the roof on all fours like a pair of playful gorillas for a few minutes shining a powerful torch on all the timbers but found nothing other than a couple of old dried out wasps nests.

The first floor bedrooms all had the same stuffy fetid aroma and were stacked high with boxes, furniture and babies. All the floors were carpeted throughout. Stitchum lifted the edge of the decaying paper thin carpet in a corner of one of the bedrooms which revealed several layers of old lino and newspaper which was now firmly stuck to the floorboards. It was quite impossible to gain access to the floorboards to carry out any sort of inspection so we moved on downstairs.   A massive assortment of junk and clutter was pulled out of the under stairs cupboard allowing Stitchum to crawl inside rather like a tenacious burrowing animal.

"Yup, it's in there I'm afraid," he called out somewhat ingenuously. As this nylon coated figure reversed out of the cupboard; the owner appeared; ashen white, and obviously preparing himself for the unpleasant news that was about to be revealed.

"Oh my God, what's in there?" he shouted in a terrified voice.

"Well, its not good news I'm afraid sir," Stitchum replied in a superbly well practiced sombre melodramatic voice. "I'm unfortunately obliged to inform you that my inspection of this property has revealed an active infestation of 'anobium punctatum' which is affecting the timbers throughout."

"Oh God, what the hell's that?" the owner enquired.

"It's actually a beetle that lays eggs in cracks and crevices in the timber. The eggs hatch and the larvae eat their way through the timbers. If it's not stopped: the house will eventually fall down. This is quite serious 'sir'; we need to treat it as a matter of extreme urgency. If I might use your telephone 'sir' I will check with our emergency teams to see how quickly they can get round here."

"Yes, yes, of course. The telephone is in here," the young sad and dispirited owner whispered in a noticeably trembling voice as he led us back into the lounge.

I felt at this point, extremely uncomfortable: very much like the witness of a callous crime that was about to be perpetrated. This in reality was exactly what was transpiring.

"Hello, is that the emergency treatment department? Its Stitchum here, I've come across a serious attack of 'anobium punctatum' in Mayfield Crescent, we need to act quickly on this one. When have you got an extermination team available? Friday…are you sure there's nothing you can do sooner than that? Only this one is really urgent...no? Alright, let me just confirm that with the customer." Placing his hand over the telephone mouthpiece, he then turned to the owner who now looked on the verge of collapse, shaking like a leaf and clearly feeling quite impotent. "Friday is the soonest 'sir'. I would have liked to have done it for you before then but there's been a whole spate of these recently all in this area."

"No, no that's fine; it won't be too late by then will it?"

"No, don't worry 'sir', we've been very fortunate and caught it just in the nick of time."

"O.K. Soakum, make that a definite booking for eight o'clock in the morning on Friday. Yes. Yes, I'll explain to the young gentleman here that he's got to get all the carpets and floor coverings up and out of the house, clear the roof out and stack all his furniture out in the garden or somewhere and remove all the babies."

"Right 'sir', that's organised. I must just ask you to sign this consent form here; we will then carry some tests to determine the presence or not as the case may be for rising dampness in the walls of this property."

It was a particularly damp and miserable day. The humidity levels inside the house were obviously very high which was no doubt exacerbated by the amount of wet nappies and baby clothes draped over the radiators and for that matter any other free surface. The windows and external walls were sodden. All the windows were of course closed which meant the ventilation was non existent. To make matters worse an un-vented tumble dryer was groaning away in the little kitchen at the rear of the house. The owner's wife a young spotty faced girl of about eleven was clutching two screaming crimson faced babies close to her bosom whilst attempting to assemble mugs of tea and biscuits for us; perhaps in the hope that we wouldn't find any further problems with the house.   A quick check Stitchum carried out with a damp meter unsurprisingly confirmed that the walls were wet. Again with the same sombre and formal tone Stitchum conveyed the bad news.

"I'm afraid I have to inform you 'sir' that tests I have today carried out on these premises confirm the presence of severe rising dampness in all the walls throughout."

"Oh god," the owner whispered to himself, now at the point of tears. "What do we have to do about that?" he asked pathetically.

"Just leave it to us 'sir' we are the experts for these sort of problems, we'll sort this out for you. When we carry out eradication treatments here on Friday, I will arrange for our specialist damp proofing technicians to install a new horizontal chemical damp proof course into all the external walls of the house."

At this point the owner's wife appeared with the tray of tea. "What will all this cost?" she said in a frightened timid child's voice.

"Well, bearing in mind the difficulties you are both facing at the moment, I shouldn't really do this: but I will arrange to install the damp course at a concessionary price, taking into account of course the fact that we shall be doing the extermination treatments at the same time."

"Yes, thank... you but what will it all cost... everything, I mean?"

"I will explain this and run through the figures now. The extermination treatments would normally be £300.00. The new damp course would normally be £600.00. Now, as we are doing the two jobs together, we will reduce the total figure to £750.00. I can't be fairer that that. To be honest I'm taking a bit of a risk knocking so much off but I can see you're not exactly awash with funds 'as it were'. There is of course V.A.T. to be added to that but there is nothing any of us can do about that."

As we were driving away, I was reflecting on what had just transpired. My thoughts were interrupted by Stitchum.

"That was a right result. Just like lambs to the slaughter," he said, grinning from ear to ear.

"Not exactly the words I would have chosen," I said caustically.

"What do you mean?" he asked.

"More like highway robbery." I clipped the words revealing my contempt. "I personally didn't look under the staircase and I really don't know if there was any woodworm there or not. Even if there was, I don't really know if it's necessary to treat the whole house. I do however know something about rising damp. The walls inside that house were literally running with water from condensation and as any damp meter works on electrical resistance it's bound to go completely off the scale. I also know that the property which had cavity brickwork had what looked to me like a pretty good damp course in the external skin of brickwork."

Stitchum went quiet, and looked quite angry. "Don't get on your high horse with me," he said aggressively.

"I'm not," I said, realising that my comments had penetrated a raw nerve.

"Look, in this game it's a case of 'dog eat dog' you can't be a Good Samaritan."

"They're not dogs; they are poor young innocent people that trusted you."

"Ah, go on like that mate and you'll have me in tears. In fact I think we ought to get the old violin out. Christ, if you've been running a building firm for so long, you must by now realise that it's a jungle out there. No one does you any favours."

"As a matter of interest...the prices you quoted, seemed high to me. Is that based on some sort of price structure?"

"Yup it surely is. It's based on the company's recommended minimum prices plus one hundred per cent. I'll explain all of that to you when we get back to the office."

"Why one hundred per cent?"

"Because basically; It was a job that had to be fitted in urgently at short notice as it were. They didn't have much choice either. The whole point is they thought they'd only got a few weeks left before a nasty man from the building society would knock on their door and ask for the keys back. In this particular instance all the valuation report for the mortgage said was that they would recommend that the owner obtains reports in respect of woodworm and damp. They didn't ask to see them. It's just a recommendation. There's no element of compulsion about it. As it happens, no one gives a toss whether they do anything about it or not. It's hardly in my interests to tell them that though is it?"

I was now quickly beginning to discover the joys of becoming a qualified home inspector for Sprayum & Scarper.

As we drove on in silence to the next 'inspection' it occurred to me that although I still felt somewhat nauseated by what had been a blatant confidence trick on a vulnerable young couple: I had perhaps been a trifle too candid and had certainly offended finer sensibilities that much to my amazement Stitchum had concealed somewhere. He was undoubtedly a bit like a child who was expecting praise for doing something clever and had got scolded instead. I convinced myself to at least see the day out and make a decision after that. In order to break the ice and lying through my teeth I said to him "Yeah, I suppose you're right in a way. I'm not trying to be difficult I just felt a bit sorry for them."

"That's all right mate don't worry about it. You're new to this game; it's bound to feel a bit strange at first. I remember when I first started. I was a right greenhorn: full of morals and principles, but that soon wears off. You've always got to remember the old saying you know: 'all is fair in love and war.' The point you've got to remember is that we're not alone. There are loads of other firms out there that are far more ruthless than us and if we don't do 'the business' one of them will. People often show us estimates and reports they've had from our competitors and you'd be bloody amazed at what they come up with. There's a lot of villains out there mate believe me."

"Isn't there some sort of regulatory body or organisation that controls the industry?"

"There certainly is mate and our 'guv'nor' is one of the committee members. It's a completely toothless organisation though: a bit like an old boys club."

"What is the name of the one that Sprayum & Scarper belong to?"

"The one they belong to is the only one really that's recognised throughout the industry it's called 'P.R.A.T.T.S'."

"What on earth does that interpret as?" I asked, assuming he was joking.

"It's 'Professional Remedial and Timber Treatment Specialists'."

"What do they actually do?"

"Not a lot is the answer to that one. The member company I think has to fulfil certain criteria before they can apply for membership. The annual turnover of the company has to be over a certain amount. The directors have to confirm that they haven't been convicted of fraud or demanding money with menaces in the twelve month period prior to applying for membership; just normal 'stuff' like that really. What actually happens if you want to join is really very much like most of these organisations: you fill in a form, send it back with a healthy old 'bung' which is what they call the application fee: a few weeks later some boozy old sod comes to see you to carry out the vetting procedure. What this basically means is that you take him out to an expensive restaurant for lunch which has to include lots of fine wines, brandy's and liqueurs

31

then afterwards: depending upon how pissed he is, you take him to visit the local knocking shop, and 'Presto' you're in. A week or so later you receive a letter of confirmation which welcomes you as a fellow 'Pratt', and permission to use the 'P.R.A.T.T.S logo on your letterheads and advertising material. This includes big gold crests that you stick on the vans saying something about 'P.R.A.T.T.S ensure excellence in the industry'. People generally are quite stupid and if they see this ornate colourful crest almost like a coat of arms they automatically assume that the company has some sort of royal charter and won't stitch them up too seriously."

"This sounds quite incredible."

"Well, you asked me, and that's how it is. If you put your hand in the glove compartment you'll find a little red book of do's and don'ts a sort of book of rules for members."

I searched around and pulled it out. 'Guide for Home Inspectors' was printed just below the red and gold crest on the front cover. Leafing through it I came across a section entitled 'the ten golden rules for house inspectors which read as follows;

'The aims of the company are set out in full in the handbook that is issued free of charge to all members. The desire of this company is to promote excellence within the industry. Each home inspector will, as a requirement by his or her employer; endeavour to achieve the highest possible standards whilst carrying out home inspections. In particular, we set out below the ten basic 'cardinal rules';

1. Inspectors must at all times ensure the highest levels of personal hygiene.
2. Inspectors must not 'stitch up' victims or 'clients' as they are sometimes called.
3. Inspectors must not request sexual favours from clients.

4.   Inspectors must not carry out an inspection whilst intoxicated.

5.   Drugs of any kind should not be taken or administered during the inspection.

6.   Violence or threats of violence should be avoided if possible. In circumstances where the client is unwilling to recognise the need to have certain works carried out, a limited degree of 'persuasion' is acceptable.

7.   Inspectors must not refer to other P.R.A.T.T. company members as 'self abusers', even though they might be quoting in competition. This particular remark can however be used where the competitor is a non P.R.A.T.T.S member.

8.   Urinating, defecating or vomiting in the clients flower beds whilst examining the location of external air bricks is forbidden at all times.

9.   Where circumstances arise, that occasion the client to express shock or dismay at the cost of any verbal estimate provided; Foul language and questioning his parentage is not permissible.

10.   Inspectors must not under any circumstances steal or 'borrow' items belonging to the client during the course of the inspection.

"Yes, quite a helpful little book really," I remarked.

"Yeah, I suppose it is really, although most of it's common sense if you think about it. It's not that dissimilar to a little book you are given in the police force. You know all the guides on questioning suspects: the permitted use of wet towels, electric shocks and that sort of thing."

"Where are we off to now?"

"This next one is a 'toff's'drum. The geezer's a retired high court judge. Right I'll take a left here and that will take us up to the private road where it is."

A short while later he stopped the car outside a large pair of black wrought iron gates set between two stone pillars.

33

Stitchum got out of the car and pressed the intercom button fixed to the one of the pillars. Sitting in the car with the door open I heard an elderly bronchial voice call out:

"Yes, who is it?"

"Good morning 'sir', it's Stitchum from Sprayum & Scarper."

I heard some throat clearing noises but couldn't work out what was said. He got back into the car; the gates slowly swung back and we drove slowly along a narrow gravel road for about three hundred yards. As the road turned a most impressive grey Victorian house came into view.

"Not a bad pile there is it?" Stitchum stated as the car came to a gentle rest outside a baronial entrance porch.

The judge: a distinguished looking grey haired fellow of about seventy greeted us rather formally and then invited us into the house.

"We seem to have rather a strange problem," he said smiling seraphically. "My wife has noticed a rather 'musty' smell in the drawing room and I thought we ought to have the experts look into it. I do hope it's nothing too serious."

"Right 'sir', a very wise decision you can never be too careful with a property like this. If you would kindly lead us to the offending room I will sniff the air in question."

"Yes indeed," the judge replied, "please follow me if you would."

The room was one of the most magnificent examples of early Victorian architecture I had ever seen, exhibiting deep intricate ornamental coving to the ceiling, high moulded skirting and half panelled walls. After acclimatising to his new surroundings, Stitchum's face took on a deathly pallor. He looked deadly serious as he took a few sniffs of the air.

"Ah yes, I do see what you mean," he said, much to my bewilderment.

"Has the property ever been treated for rising damp?"

"No, not as far as I am aware," the judge replied, "we have been here for nearly forty years and it certainly hasn't in that time for I should jolly well know about it."

"Right 'sir' I have reason to suspect that the somewhat offensive nature of this unpleasant odour is that of rising damp. I will now proceed to get some test equipment from my vehicle whereupon I will, with your permission carry out a few investigative test procedures."

"That's very kind of you," said the judge trying to smile, and undoubtedly feeling slightly perplexed by Stitchum's instant diagnosis.

In virtually no time he had returned clutching two damp meters: one had a lead attached to it with two metal prongs fixed to the end of it. This meter gave a reading on a large calibrated dial. The other which seemed to alarm the judge considerably had a lead coming from it which was attached to a small sensor pad. This meter was far more dramatic and disturbing in that it made an extremely unpleasant and urgent screeching sound.

"Oh dear," the judge commented. "That doesn't sound good."

"No 'sir' you're quite right, it isn't good. I'm afraid this property is actually suffering from severe rising dampness throughout."

"Oh dear," the judge whispered once again, "what do you suggest?"

"In this situation 'sir' there is only one thing that can be done," he said, pausing for a few moments to allow the judge to assimilate the bad news. "We will have to install a new horizontal chemical damp proof course in all the external walls."

A predictable, 'oh dear' was followed by 'oh dear' again as the judge shook his head obviously fearing the worst. "Is it going to be very disruptive?" he asked.

"No 'sir' not at all. Our highly trained technicians are experts in these matters. They'll do all the work from outside with no internal disruption whatsoever. It will of course be a little noisy for a few days but we can't do anything about that."

"Well, I suppose you had better let me have an estimate then if you would be so kind. Will this cure the musty smell my wife's going on about?"

"Oh yes you'll never be troubled by this noxious odour again and on completion of the work you will receive a thirty year guarantee to give you complete peace of mind. I just need to take some measurements outside after which, I will be able to let you know the total cost."

Once outside, Stitchum suggested that the musty smell was probably the judges' wife.

"I reckon she's been dead for years and he doesn't even realize," he stated.

After a close inspection of the flower beds and a few abortive attempts to measure the outside of the property, Stitchum was calling out "excuse me 'sir' are you there?"

"Ah, did you get on all right?" the judge enquired as he appeared from an entrance at the rear, "do come back inside it really is quite chilly out here today."

"Thank you 'sir', I have now been able to ascertain the total cost of all this which is exactly six grand . . . sorry, I mean six thousand pounds."

"Oh dear, that is far more than I'd ever imagined, I really need to think about this."

"Well, actually, 'sir' I was just about to say to you, if we can fit this in with a very large job we will be doing a few roads away I can offset quite a bit of the cost. In fact on that basis I would be able to offer you a fifty per cent discount."

"That is extremely kind of you," said the judge, "I would still like to think about it and discuss it with my wife."

"Well 'sir' with respect that is really your choice. The only thing I must tell you is that I can't keep the offer open after today. This afternoon we will be ordering the materials for this other big job we are starting and I was going to include the materials for this in the order."

"Yes, yes, it really is most kind of you, and I really do appreciate your concern but I would like a little time to think on it."

"Well 'sir' if I may say so don't think on it for too long. The tests I have carried out here this morning indicate beyond any doubt that this property is in imminent danger of developing dry rot. The stagnant air trapped behind this panelling and the brickwork is an ideal breeding ground for dry rot spores. It would be terrible if you had to rip this entire lot out," he said pointing to the wall panelling. "Three grand, I mean three thousand pounds would soon end up being thirty. The price I have offered you is just to cover our labour. I'm virtually throwing the materials in for nothing."

"Oh look, yes, please do it for me as quickly as you can. I do apologise for dithering: I think this is one of the problems when one gets older you know."

"Just sign here 'sir', this will hold that figure for you and confirm the booking. Our work planning department will contact you in the next few days to arrange a start date. Well thank you again 'sir' you can now relax knowing you have made a very wise decision."

Back in the car Stitchum looked over at me trying to suppress another broad grin. "It's just like falling off a log eh?" he said. "Two down, two to go."

I didn't really need to ask any more questions. It had become quite clear what was required if I were to succeed in my new post. If I could stand it, I thought it might be interesting to learn more about this loathsome industry. I had like most builders always been sceptical about these company's activities and I realised now it wasn't without some justification. I knew for a fact that I would be both unable and unwilling, to employ the sort of tactics I had witnessed that were an integral part of Stitchum's sales technique; and presumably all the other house inspectors not just those employed by this company, but the thousands of other similar enterprises. Still these were early days; at least that's what I kept saying to myself knowing really that my first assessment of the situation was absolutely correct.

"This one we're going to now's a key job" Stitchum said. "If you look at the job sheet on the dashboard there you'll see it's a 1930's semi. They're always definite jobs; they all follow the same pattern. It's going to be a youngish couple; probably second time buyers; almost certainly sold a flat somewhere because of kids, or kids on the way, that sort of thing and needing a whopping great mortgage. On these the building societies virtually always insist on seeing a report and a guarantee before they release the money. It's definitely going to have woodworm that's not in question. The problem is how many other quotes are they getting?"

He stopped the car abruptly outside an estate agents office. "Quick, run in there and ask for the keys of 62 Pinewood Avenue," he shouted urgently as if it was a matter of life or death.

I ran in for the keys as instructed, explained it was for a woodworm inspection and was handed a large bunch of keys. No questions were asked, no proof of identity requested, nothing. They had certainly never seen me before. Fortunate for the owners I thought that in this case my intentions were honourable . . . well, almost.

When we arrived at the property, we had a quick look in the roof to see if there were any stored items up there and to check on the insulation. Stitchum explained that whenever possible they try to persuade the customer to remove any insulation before the spraying of the timbers is carried out. The only reason for this is that it makes the job easier and quicker for the operative. We were unable, in the short time that we were in the roof space to see any signs of woodworm. The floors were completely covered with fitted carpets. It didn't actually make much difference anyway, because he had already decided there was an active attack of 'anobium punctatum' everywhere. I was told the best way to deal with this as far as securing the contract goes was to telephone the client and try and find out how many other quotes they have had; who they are from, and what sort of figures were being quoted. Then we would get some idea of how to 'pitch' it.

We dropped the keys back to the agents and headed on towards our fourth and final inspection of the morning. It was now just after midday and Stitchum was becoming anxious that we must get it done in time for lunch. This was a very small late Victorian terraced house on a busy main road. The proposed purchasers, our clients; obviously young first time buyers according to Stitchum; had experienced problems in obtaining a mortgage on the property as the valuer acting for their building society had found extensive dampness in the ground floor. Any mortgage offer was going to be conditional upon damp and timber reports being obtained and then being submitted to the building society.

"These can be tricky," he explained, "chances are they're pot less. In most cases like this they will get half a dozen quotes in the hope that some half wit will go in there and do the job for nothing. You can guarantee they will want a ninety nine per cent mortgage on it and the building society is almost certainly going to make a retention of the amount they lend. What that means is that if we got the job, our price will have been the lowest. We would then have to do all the work; probably while their living there and then when it's finished: wait God knows how long for the building society's surveyor to come and check it before the cheque's released. You also have to make damn sure the cheque is made payable to us and not to them."

"Not exactly an attractive proposition then?" I said rather pointlessly.

"Exactly so. At least we're on the same planet now."

We pulled up on double yellow lines outside the house. The property was coated in a black greasy traffic film and had a rusty old dismantled motor cycle in the tiny paved front garden. The bottom panel of the glazed front door had been kicked in and was now covered by pieces of brown cardboard that had been taped around it. On the top panel of the door was a warning notice with a picture of an angry looking dog in the centre. Below this were written the words 'Vicious Dog Lives Here' 'Bites First, Asks Questions After'. Stitchum knocked on the door, the noise of which signalled the dog's attention. This was evidenced by some blood curdling yelping and growling: lots of shouting and screaming could be heard from inside the house. I stepped a few paces back in the hope of retaining all of my limbs. The door or what was left of it opened revealing a frightening looking woman of about forty with the most enormous unsupported frontal appendages. The dog, a Staffordshire bull terrier, was snarling menacingly bearing its highly dangerous looking teeth but was being held back by the woman's black and blue varicose leg which firmly pressed the dog's body against the door frame.

"What the bloody hell do you want?" she screamed in a voice that sent a shiver through me.

"We're from Sprayum and Scarper love; we've come to carry . . ."

"Oh no you're bloody not," she interrupted before he could get the sentence out.

"I thought our office had phoned you to arrange this appointment," he said rather sheepishly.

"No one's phoned me and you're bloody well not coming in 'ere, I've 'ad five of your lot round 'ere this week. You can bugger off, go on, sling your 'ook, or I'll let the 'bleedin dog go."

The snarling dog was kicked backed inside and the door slammed shut.

"Good God, how many do you come across like that?" I asked as we got back into the car.

"Not that many, but now you can probably see what I was saying. These stupid people ask half a dozen or more companies to go out and do estimates for them, basically

40

because it's a free inspection: but they don't give a thought to the aggravation or inconvenience it creates for the vendor."

It was now about twelve thirty. Not enough time to go back and do anything at the office and too soon to go to a cafe for lunch because of the strict time embargo. The next thirty minutes were spent sitting in the car enjoying a stimulating discussion on the vile mating habits of the common furniture beetle and Stitchum's worsening erectile dysfunction.

Chapter Three

The atmosphere inside the crowded little cafe was stifling. The humidity was intense with constant jets of steam being released and billowing up to the ceiling from a large chrome tea urn behind the counter. The relentless clatter of cutlery, crockery, pots and pans, coupled with the hot stuffy grease laden air; the raucous shouting and general banter, gave me an almost instant headache. I had an overwhelming desire to flee and escape to the fresh air. Watching Stitchum frantically devour a massive pile of greasy fried eggs, bacon, chips, sausages and beans all covered in gigantic dollops of brown sauce and tomato ketchup was not a pleasant experience. The knife and fork he worked with were held in clench fists as if he were thumb less. This mountain of saturated fat disappeared so quickly that I still had only half eaten the ham roll that I had ordered by the time he'd finished and threw the knife and fork on to his plate. He then ate four large slices of bread and butter which was swilled down with a large mug of tea. For a few moments I was transfixed observing a small part of a chip coated in tomato ketchup that had been ejected with some considerable force by Stitchum in his panic to scoop the food in quickly enough, and this was slowly sliding down the side of my mug of tea. Suspecting that he had noticed my interest in this and not wishing to embarrass him I tried to divert his attention.

"Don't you get indigestion eating that quickly?" I asked him.

"No course not, there's no point in fannying around with food. If you want it get it down your neck that's what I say," he replied, wiping his mouth with the back of his hand and releasing a terrifying belch.

"Aren't you going to eat that?" he said looking at my half eaten ham roll.

"No, no, I'm not really hungry."

He picked it up and in two mouthfuls it was gone.

"Right, let's get back to the office. We've got to get these reports written up and we'll get some stuff together for you to read up on. I'm going to do a little detour on the way back and drop in at a job that's in progress just to make sure its going alright."

"What's the job?" I enquired.

"Oh it's just a floor replacement. It's one of mine. They started it last week and it should be just about wrapped by now."

After some serious belching and some other fairly unpleasant bodily noises the car was started and we headed towards 'the job'.

"What do you do with yourself in the evenings?" he enquired as another extended and rather tuneful belch was released.

"Why do you ask?"

"Well, because you are going to have to put some time in. You've got a fair bit to learn you know."

"What about in particular?"

"For a start you've got all the Latin names of the beetles, and not just them. You've got to learn all the Latin names for the various forms of rot."

"Why is it necessary to know the Latin names for them?" I asked.

"Good question really, well no . . . The answer's quite simple. The idea is that it gives the punter the impression that you've had some sort of scientific background and training, so that the diagnosis you come up with appears to be based on some sort of research into entomology and mycology. You know the branches of science that deal with insects and fungi. Telling someone they've got an infestation of 'Anobium Punctatum' is far more impressive than just saying 'you've just got a bit of woodworm.' This is particularly true with wet rot and dry rot. If you explain to someone that they've got a bit of dry rot, they'll probably turn the other cheek if you know what I mean. What you have to do is present the case to them very seriously. Take them aside and then give them the business."

"What do you mean by that?" I asked, already really knowing what he meant.

"The only way to describe it I suppose, is a bit like a doctor with a patient. If the doctor has to give the patient some bad news, say the patients got cancer: he doesn't just blurt it out in a jovial voice. He gets very serious, starts using all these Greek and Latin medical words knowing that the poor bugger he's talking to hasn't got a clue what's wrong with him; only that it's probably *not just* a touch of flu. It's the same with us; we're like doctors, sort of house doctors, if you get my drift. So when you come across a bit of rot somewhere and say for example its dry rot, you say to the customer something like 'I'm very sorry to have to tell you that my inspection of this property has revealed an outbreak of 'Serpula Lacrymans'; and that mate, puts the fear of God in them whether their church goers or not."

"Strange really," I replied, "I'm actually surprised people fall for that. I thought Latin was a bit of a dead language or something that was only used in the legal and medical professions."

"No mate, no, it's alive and kicking in this game and I tell you what we'd all probably be on the dole without it. So you might say that the geezer who invented it is worth his weight in fungicide."

We had only been in the cafe for about fifteen minutes in total but the vile sickly stench of old chip fat permeated the

44

car. I now understood why the 'inspectors' room had the same obnoxious odour. As we drove around the dismal and depressing suburbs of Southampton heading towards 'the job', I was wondering how much longer I could stand of this. 'Just stay with it, only a few hours to go, and that's the first day over with', I kept thinking to myself.

"This is the one," he said, the last word being amalgamated with a further muffled belch, as he drew up behind a Sprayum & Scarper van parked half on the road and half on the pavement. The property was a red brick Edwardian semi which had been reasonably well maintained. The small front garden was piled high with old timbers that instead of being stacked neatly in some sort of fashion were in a heap much resembling a bonfire. Bags of rubbish and building debris were strewn about all over the remainder of the garden and the pathway leading up to the entrance door. Underneath the mountain of old timber one could see in places that there was a neatly trimmed square of grass with flower borders around the edge. The plants and flowers that could just be seen had been broken and crushed by the debris thrown over them. We climbed over this obstacle course and walked in to the front reception room where there were two quite unsavoury and cretinous looking oiks. One, a long haired unshaven fellow of about twenty five was sitting on part of the newly 'constructed' floor eating a bag of crisps. The other, who was probably a few years younger, was equally dishevelled with a cigarette hanging from his mouth while he attempted to cut a section of floorboard which was precariously balanced over the client's coffee table. Without looking at the work which had hitherto been 'completed' it was immediately evident that this fellow wasn't a carpenter. Stitchum asked him how they were getting on which produced a plethora of complaints, expletives, abuse and general moaning about the house, the client, his tools, the quality of the timber and the time that had been allowed for the job: the list was interminable.

45

A quick look around at the work they had completed revealed quite clearly that neither of them had a clue as to how to go about things. They patently had no proper skills whatsoever between the two of them. The new floor joists instead of being supported on timber plates, were propped up with old bricks which had been laid directly on to the soil of the oversite. The new floorboards, fixed over these were covered in 'half crowns' or dents where on driving the nails in they had carried on hitting the spot where the nail was causing an indentation the shape of the hammer head in the new boards. Many of them were split and not one of them had anything remotely resembling a straight saw cut on the ends or where one floorboard abutted another. The whole floor was considerably out of level and what flooring had been laid dropped and creaked as I stood on it.

"We aint genna finish this today," the oik with the saw advised.

"What do you mean?" Stitchum replied aggressively.

"Nuffink's right abart this bleeding job. The bloke's wot built this ouse dint know wot they was doing. We won't never finish it. We've ad all sorts of aggro just tryin to get it level, know wot I mean? We ad to spend alf a day just levelling it up like."

"Well it's got to be finished," Stitchum said sternly.

"Look mate, the other one said, who had now finished his crisps and was standing up, "we've worked ard on this and we can't work bleeding miracles."

After much arguing, swearing and shouting we left with Stitchum having the last word.

"If it's not completed today the job you are both on tomorrow will have to be put back. If that happens I'll have to explain to the guv'nors that you both haven't been pulling your weight. You both know very well what that would mean. If you want to be unemployed a few weeks before Christmas that's up to you. If not, my advice to both of you is to get off your backsides and get it finished."

Stitchum, who was now quite red in the face, released another fearsome belch as we got back into the car.

The first ten minutes of our drive back to the office was taken up with Stitchum employing just about every possible adjective and expletive he could think of to confirm and further express his annoyance and dislike of these two operatives. The loud gastro intestinal noises became much more frequent. I was now wondering if he had perhaps considered the question I had posed to him earlier about indigestion.

"Doesn't the company employ carpenters for this sort of work?" I asked him.

"No, they don't. They won't pay the rates for skilled trades and anyway all the operatives do a bit of everything. After all you don't need to be a builder or a carpenter to take an old floor out and lay a new one, do you?"

"Yes, I think is the answer to that one. Don't people ever complain?" I asked caustically.

"What do you mean?"

"The standard of work, they are trying to do is appalling." I stated, quite amazed that he seemed unaware of this.

"Oh, come on its not that bad" he proffered in their defence. "They should have finished it by now though. That's when people complain: when you tell them a job's going to be finished on a certain day and it's not; that's when they start whining."

"You mean they don't they don't mind the new floor being 'butchered' and 'cowboyed' as long as its finished on time?"

"Yeah, I see where you're coming from," he replied: obviously still not completely understanding what I meant. "It's probably different for you and the game you've been in. Being a carpenter and builder, no doubt you can see lots of little details that maybe are not quite right. Most people are delighted about having a new floor; they don't notice these things. Do you understand what I'm saying?"

47

"Yes, I do unfortunately."

"What's that supposed to mean?" he asked whilst his face contorted grotesquely whilst further gasses were released.

"We're not talking about 'little details' here. The floor isn't just 'not quite right', nothing about it is anywhere near right, it's an absolute travesty." I could feel myself becoming quite angry with this pointless discussion. It was now my turn to start getting red in the face.

"Oh well mate, let us not let ourselves get into a state over it," he said patronisingly, "ours is not the reason why."

The point I was trying to make was completely lost on him. He clearly didn't understand or perhaps didn't want to understand. What annoyed me most of all was that 'the firm'; for the money they were charging, could have employed two carpenters to carry out the work properly. They'd still have made a massive profit on the price that was quoted. I knew that I could have carried out the work properly for half the money and in half the time and still would have made a generous profit. The two characters who were working there couldn't in all honesty be blamed. They probably thought they'd worked hard and had done their best, but had in reality absolutely no idea of how to go about it and no skills between the two of them.

I later learned that of all the fourteen operatives employed: None of them had a trade or any proper skills at all. According to Stitchum they were all 'practical' whatever that meant and most of them could ominously 'turn their hands to anything'. They were all paid a pittance and were continually being threatened and intimidated by the hierarchy.

One thing now I had realised beyond any doubt was that the likelihood of me ever actually working for this company as a house inspector was even more remote. If I could somehow manage to refrain from making sarcastic comments about the Machiavellian system which was basically driving this enterprise: If I were also able to persuade myself that it was in order to sell somebody a new floor for example, that they didn't actually need . . . I would then have to accept warnings, threats and monies deducted from me when the incompetent unskilled monkey's that do the job, mess it up completely, fail to complete it on time or probably both. To try and endure this would undoubtedly be beyond any acceptable boundaries of sanity. So having spotted this minor little drawback I decided that as there was nothing else in the offing I would carry on for a further few hours and complete the first day.

When we walked into the 'inspector's room', the other three scoundrels were huddled in the far corner smoking, drinking tea and exchanging stories all of which were on similar lines, namely trying to elevate themselves into being the sharpest, wiliest, and most proficient amongst their number. Stitchum immediately joined in the competition, which on this occasion produced no immediately obvious winner although it was a close run thing between his story of the judge with the 'musty' smell and the encounter that Robbum related, which was without doubt in their eyes a close runner up.

"It was like this," Robbum started; "I had this roof to look at one of those small rat holes on the Portsmouth Road. Bugger all up there; all those roofs were constructed with redwood. I've never seen worm in them yet. Anyway, I parked the car and walked carrying my ladder and the torch about half a bleeding mile to the house in the drizzle; soaked to the skin by the time I got there. It turns out that a young couple's bought it and they've just got a recommendation that the roof should be checked for woodworm. If the numbskull carrying out the valuation for the building society knew his arse from his elbow, he would have known that these properties never have worm in the roof timbers. A quick look around up there confirmed exactly that. The only thing was, they'd put an old tea chest up there when they moved in a few weeks before. Around the top of this there were some old flight holes and I mean old, probably older than me and that's saying something. Anyway I called the woman and asked her to come up in the roof and showed her the holes. I explained that these houses don't normally have woodworm, but as they'd brought in an item that was 'infested' with the larvae the chances were that they will have crawled out and laid hundreds of eggs everywhere in the roof. She actually screamed with fright at the very thought of all these little things crawling about above her bedroom. I told her the tea chest must be taken out immediately and burned and that we would need to spray all the roof timbers with a powerful insecticide as a precautionary measure. I even helped her to get the tea chest out of the roof."

He then paused for a few seconds, with a self satisfied grin, giving the listeners a chance to assimilate the sagacious proficiency of his performance.

"That's not the half it," he continued, "it was still only half a day to spray the roof: nothing to get too excited about so as I left I knocked on her neighbour's doors either side. I explained that the lady that had just moved in had got woodworm. Well not the lady herself; the roof of the house she had just bought and out of courtesy I felt it was my duty to advise them so that they would have the opportunity of having theirs treated at a discounted rate. I explained how quickly these 'infestations' can spread and the damage they can do, and they couldn't sign the acceptance forms quick enough."

The stories the other two regaled ran along similar lines but were less creative and imaginative than the other two. It became readily apparent that for all of them, far more pleasure and satisfaction was derived from selling treatments that were unnecessary, as opposed to ones that were. The only exception to this seemed to be where they had submitted an estimate for some treatments that were actually required, and were about to lose the job because a competitors quote was cheaper than theirs. This scenario occurred frequently and a number of ruses were used to win the client over which ranged from confidently advising the client that the competitor firm was about to go into liquidation and the guarantee they issued would be worthless. To explaining in the strictest confidence of course, that people had found personal items missing after their operatives had recently carried out work in the vicinity. A further devious ruse employed was to suggest discretely that the operatives working for that particular company always diluted the chemicals used with water in order to use only half the amount designated for each particular job. They then, it was said, sold the rest of the chemical to supplement their income.

"Right, enough of this 'fannying' around," Stitchum stated assertively: "we've got to draft these reports out. Here grab a seat," he said, pulling one of the old upholstered dining chairs across the battered old desk we had been sitting on.

The report writing was far simpler than I had imagined. The woodworm reports comprised of a few numbered paragraphs that corresponded to what was programmed on their word processors. Paragraph one, was the opening one for the report. Number two confirmed the inspection was carried out, and detailed what areas were inspected. Number three states what treatments are proposed, and number four, the price. The whole report could be written out in under a minute. Despite Stitchum's insistence that there was a lot to learn, I didn't find this particular exercise too onerous. The damp proofing reports were prepared along similar lines and with these it was necessary to draw a little sketch plan of the walls that were to be treated and then place crosses along the length of them wherever the damp readings were found. You had to write in other details such as whether the internal wall plaster had to be removed and to what height plus any other relevant details. The reports for dry rot, wet rot, timber renewals etc, were all equally simple. I found it difficult to understand why it was a six week training course. The only other areas we had not really touched upon were to do with identifying the various kinds of wood rot. As there were only two of them that really mattered; wet rot and dry rot; it certainly wasn't going to be too difficult. It was of course much easier for me having building experience. I already knew about the various kinds of wood rot, where damp courses are located, and of course all about timber renewals. The price structure was so well thought out that it was virtually idiot proof which without casting too many aspersions, it needed to be. I was given an inspectors handbook which contained all the various bits of information with a list of examples. These included the cost of spraying roof spaces for various sized houses, the cost of spraying floors and the price per square metre for damp courses, hacking off plaster and replastering. There were also prices listed for dry rot sterilization of masonry and colourful photographs of dry rot sporophores, which looked like large pizzas   This hand book also listed the time it should take to take up and replace a rotted timber floor with illustrations showing the right way and the wrong way of doing it with pictorial sketches of happy faced 'Mister Men' caricatures in boiler suits holding pieces of timber. I showed Stitchum these pictures whilst remarking that the two fellows we saw earlier on didn't really look like this and perhaps that was why the floor wasn't finished.   But for some obscure reason he was not amused.

Cheatum, the unsavoury looking character; was now sitting opposite us making telephone calls to would be purchasers of properties he had inspected, whilst the other three were drafting out their reports. I was supposedly studying the company's price structure and trying to memorize the Latin names of various beetles. My attention was diverted by the telephone conversation that was taking place opposite; which started as follows:

"Good afternoon sir, is that Mr Brown? Oh excellent, it's Cheatum here from Sprayum & Scarper. How are you today sir? Oh good, good, pleased to hear it sir. Now, I'm pleased that I've been able to catch you sir as it is a matter of some importance. I gather you haven't exchanged contracts on 42 Mulberry Avenue yet. No, oh that's excellent news sir. I was worried that things might have moved quickly without you being aware of certain problems that I have discovered. Well what it is: I know your building society mentioned that you should have the roof checked for woodworm and that's what I checked first of al, and you really can't miss it up there sir, it almost jumps out and bites you as it were. Whenever there's an infestation in the roof void we always inspect the floors as these things can spread through a building at an alarming rate as I am sure you understand sir. Now the first floors are quite sound except for some eggs I came across under the floorboards of the front bedroom. Yes sir that's right they are very small, virtually invisible to the naked eye, but unlike other less professional companies we use special equipment to search for these. Yes sir, that's absolutely right sir, both the roof and the first floors will need spraying with a powerful insecticide. Oh no sir, Oh no, the chemical we use is quite harmless, oh no, it's absolutely harmless sir, what do we use? Did I hear you ask? Well it's a sort of nerve agent. No, I don't believe it's a painful death at all. Well certainly none of them have ever complained about it sir. Yes, yes, I will be sending you an estimate for that but there is something else sir; I'm really sorry to have to tell you this but I really wouldn't be doing my job properly if I ignored it. Well sir, on checking the ground floor timbers I found some 'Coniophora Puteana' in the sub floor timbers of the rear reception room. No I'm sure you haven't heard of it sir. It's a fungal disease of timber. Yes it *will* be fairly expensive sir and I know it's the last thing you need at a stressful time like this that's why I needed to speak to you as soon as possible. I've literally just walked into my office this second and said to my secretary 'I must make a phone call before I do anything'. Not at all sir, no problem sir . . . about two and half grand in total sir, yes I will get that in the post to your straight away sir, no, no, my pleasure, the least I can do under the circumstances, thank you sir, goodbye, goodbye."

"YES, Cheatum shouted, punching the air after he'd slammed the phone down; his face contorting into an, angry terrifying expression. YES, got im."

We had all being listening intently to this conversation somewhat bemused and anxious to know the outcome.

"He's an evil bugger," Trickum stated, as he wiped some rotting food debris from his long drooping moustache with the back of his hand. "He'd rob his own mother given half a chance."

"Was there anything there?" Robbum enquired.

Cheatum then turned around grinning obsequiously. "Would I lie to anyone?" he asked, and released a gross self satisfied chuckle. "Nah, it was clean as a whistle. Some old flight holes in the roof. I couldn't look at the floors; thick fitted carpets laid everywhere. There was a little bit of movement in the back room downstairs, could have been a joist end or a bit of rot in the wall plate, something like that. Or maybe it was my imagination," he said grinning again. "The thing is buying a house is the biggest decision most people ever make in their lives. You can't take chances; always err on the side of caution, that's the motto of the company is it not?"

"Quite right," Robbum confirmed. "Well done mate."

One of the most perplexing things I found was that these 'inspectors' were not exactly blessed with sophistication, subtlety or charm. It seemed to me that most people should have given them a very wide berth, but this would not seem to be the case. Without being unduly unkind, they all seemed to have some difficulty in stringing a simple sentence together. The combination of a certain devious animal cunning, the use of a few Latin words they had somehow managed to remember, along with the air of confidence and authority they exuded; enabled them to exploit people on quite a phenomenal scale.

Chapter Four

I realised fairly quickly that what feeds and perpetuates this dubious industry, is the ignorance of chartered surveyors who carry out valuations for building society's and other lending institutions. Most chartered surveyors know little or nothing about beetle infestation, wood rot or rising dampness. According to Stitchum, he hadn't met one yet who knew his arse from his elbow. Because of the ever increasing greedy compensation culture that is now endemic in our society; surveyors themselves through lack of any proper knowledge, training or understanding of such problems, will always 'err' on the side of caution. Another factor of course is the fact that most of them are inherently lazy, and are certainly not interested in getting their soft manicured hands dirty. The great majority of chartered surveyors would certainly react in horror and incredulity if they were asked to crawl around inside a roof space or take up a floorboard in order to carry out a sub floor timber inspection. Virtually all of the valuations carried out for mortgage purposes are undertaken by surveyors donned in expensive suits. Not exactly 'de rigueur' for doing anything useful. As a consequence of this whether it is due to laziness, ignorance or self protection, or quite possibly all three: the majority of valuations for mortgage purposes and for that matter home buyers reports, and full building surveys, will always contain a paragraph, or at least a few lines suggesting that a specialist company is employed to carry out a timber and damp inspection, and on cavity constructed properties of a certain age; a cavity wall tie inspection. Whether there happens to be a genuine problem or whether as in most cases, there is no woodworm, rot, or dampness, the very fact that a so called 'professional' has suggested an inspection is carried out; is exactly the cue the home inspector needs. 'He wouldn't have put that clause in your mortgage valuation 'sir', if he didn't suspect there was a problem', is the sales pitch used by the inspectors at Sprayum & Scarper, and for that matter all the other hyena's throughout the country.

I knew from many years in the building trade that most treatments carried out for woodworm in this country are totally unnecessary. Most woodworm holes or 'flight holes' as they are called are historic. Whenever a surveyor sees these they normally suggest that there is an infestation of woodworm even though in the majority of cases the beetle has long since departed, but has not been considerate enough to fill the hole that's just been bored by his emergence from the timber. Unless these holes are fresh with sharp well defined edges and there is some evidence of fresh bore dust around the exit hole, they will almost certainly be literally just old woodworm holes.

Thankfully now the day was drawing to a close. The inspectors had phoned their various victims and had completed the draft reports which were all taken to the typing pool ready for the next day's production. The conversation now revolved around football, what they were going to have for 'tea', and of course Stitchum's erectile dysfunction, which he clearly now regretted divulging to them. It was now a quarter to five and looking quite dark outside with gusts of wind and light rain hitting the windows. Suddenly the door opened and TM appeared: said nothing, but walked slowly and menacingly towards the back of the room where we were seated. I couldn't quite be sure if it was a controlled smirk on his grey face or a wince of pain. He carried his giant cumbersome bulk down the isle between the desks and stopped just in front of where Stitchum and I were seated.

"Well", he said looking at me, "how did you get on?"

"Okay I think," I replied, not knowing what sort of a response he expected.

"What does that mean?"

"Stitchum's an excellent tutor."

"I've never heard him called that before," he said, which caused loud guffaws of guttural moronic laughter from the others.

"Have you sold any deals?" he asked me, exhibiting the strange smirk once more.

"Still learning the ropes at the moment," I replied.

"Of course," he said in a far more conciliatory tone, "you can't know it all in ten minutes."

"Actually it won't take him long," Stitchum intervened, "a few weeks I should imagine: he knows all the building side of it."

"Good," TM stated, "we need to get some action going in Brighton as soon as possible, so the quicker you can get to grips with it the better," he said, giving me the same cold penetrating look I remembered from the interview.

Driving back to Brighton through the pouring rain, I was finding it difficult to suppress my feelings of anger and injustice at a system that allowed charlatan companies like Sprayum and Scarper to survive and prosper whilst small genuine businesses like my own offering genuine advice, first class workmanship and value for money, should be driven out of business.

That evening, deciding to think positively, I drank a bottle of wine and then concentrated on learning the Latin names of the various beetles. There were eight of them listed in the handbook but the two most common were Anobium Punctatum, (common furniture beetle) being the one everyone refers to as 'woodworm, and 'Xestobium Rufovillosum', the death watch beetle. The others were weevils that attack timber that basically has already been pre digested by the wet rot fungus, and a bark boring beetle that lives on any bark that might remain on a section of cut timber. There was something quite rare called 'A house longhorn beetle.' I found a magnified picture of this one quite disturbing. Something possibly to do with the sinister expression on its face.

By midnight that evening, after a greasy Chinese takeaway I was able to recite the names and the Latin equivalents of all of these beetles from which I derived a perverse form of pleasure and satisfaction. I now had to learn and remember details of their strange life styles and revolting mating habits. For me, if I were to continue with this 'training course', the ultimate humiliation would be failing to pass the exam at the end of it. I now had the possibility of five hours beetle free sleep before setting off at six o'clock in the morning for a further exciting and enthralling episode.

On my arrival at Sprayum & Scarper's offices the next morning I found Stitchum engaged in what appeared to be a grave crisis meeting with Soakum who looked terrible: his face was a combination of blue and scarlet. It was difficult to discern where his eyes were as they blended in with the rest of his facial colouring. The stale fumes of beer and spirits pervaded the fetid atmosphere of the inspector's room. The problem evidently was that Stitchum's floor replacement job had predictably not been finished, despite the threats promulgated by him the previous day. Both operatives that were working on it were now due at another job where new skirting needed to be fitted after some damp proofing and replastering works had just been completed. Soakum couldn't take the operatives off the over running floor job as the owners had already complained after having to postpone their return to the house. The owner of the other property, requiring the new skirting was a friend of Andrew Stone and it was absolutely imperative that the completion of this went ahead smoothly, otherwise, using Soakum's words 'all hell would be let loose'. After a little more head scratching Stitchum came up with the solution;

"Clive, would you do us a favour mate?"

"Is the skirting on the site?" I asked obviously not needing to ask what the favour was.

"Yup, it was all dropped off there yesterday," Soakum confirmed.

"I need some tools; I don't have anything with me." I told them.

"I'll soon sort that out," Soakum said looking mightily relieved, "I'll be back in a moment; I'm just going to have forage around and see what I can get together. If Stitchum then drops you of at the job: you can work out how much time its going to take you and then he can pick you up again when it's finished."

"Fine, that's no problem," I said, trying unsuccessfully to conceal my lack of enthusiasm.

A few minutes later we were heading towards the job. When we arrived we were greeted initially by a pleasant, but obviously highly strung woman in her mid thirties who showed us into the front reception room which was now a through lounge. The wall plaster to all the walls had been hacked off to a height of about one metre; presumably a new damp course had been installed, and the walls replastered. The furniture was piled up high in the centre of the room and was covered in dust and plaster 'snots'. It was quite evident that the stress and inconvenience of having this work carried out had obviously been too much for her.

"This is Clive, our carpenter," Stitchum explained to her. "All he's got to do this morning is to fit new skirting and then we'll be out of your hair."

"Oh thank god for that," the woman exclaimed, "this has been has been the worst nightmare I could have ever imagined. I'm not being rude, but I just can't wait for you people to finish and go. I don't know how long it's going to take me, but I can't wait to get my house into some sort of order again."

"If you give me about two hours that should do it," I advised Stitchum.

"Right, thanks mate; I'll shoot off, I'll knock off the first two inspections and call back."

As soon as he left I had a close look at what had euphemistically been referred to as plastering and couldn't quite believe how bad it was. Where the new plaster joined the old at about one metre high, it was about half an inch proud all around the room. The new plaster had been trowelled over the existing wall paper that no one had bothered to remove. The front covers of the power points had been removed, and the metal boxes behind them were completely filled with sand, cement and plaster. At the junction of the floor boards and the wall, the rendering and plaster 'bellied' out several inches away from the wall finish. I held a reasonably straight piece of the new skirting against the new plastering which showed that at floor level the dips and hollows were far more pronounced. It really was going to be physically impossible to fix skirting against this. I realized the delicate nature of the situation and was trying to decide on the most diplomatic way to extricate myself with the minimum collateral damage.

"Do you take milk and sugar?" I heard a strained tense voice call from the kitchen.

"Erm, yes, both please, two sugars."

I knew very well that all the 'plastering' that had been carried out would all have to be completely hacked off and redone. It seemed so unjust to me that I should have to be the one to break the news to her, particularly as she was clearly on the verge of a complete nervous breakdown from what had transpired hitherto.

"There you are, I'll leave it here it here on the window cill," she said, placing a mug of tea on the plaster splattered cill.

"Actually, there appears to be a slight problem here," I said cautiously, causing her to turn around and come back into the room."

"Oh no, not more problems, what is it now?" She asked in a quivering strained voice.

"There's a slight problem with the plastering. I think the plasterers will need to come back."

"You've got to be joking," she screamed, "right that's it, I've had enough. I'm getting straight on to 'your' firm now. When my husband hears about this there'll be heads rolling," she shrieked.

Deciding that enough was enough; I left her shrieking obscenities down the telephone and made a hasty exit leaving the few tools I had been given on the floor. I certainly couldn't wait there until Stitchum returned so I decided to walk back to the office, trying of course to remember in which direction it was.

I had only been back at the office for ten minutes when Stitchum arrived looking extremely distressed. Andrew the psychopath, stormed towards him, before he could say anything to me, Andrew said to him "Right, I want to see you in my office, now," and at the same time gave me a piercing murderous angry look. The description of psychopath although not entirely appropriate, was understandable. He did certainly exhibit a rather unnerving countenance. What contributed to this was the fact that his bright green eyes were spaced unusually far apart on his face. One, the right one, appeared to be sited slightly higher, and at an angle to the other. A short ginger beard concealed his small mouth which transformed itself from a smile to a grimace in micro seconds. He never appeared to be totally relaxed and in many ways reminded me of a trapped frightened animal that was about to leap. He was not particularly tall: about five foot nine, but moved like a cheetah on speed.

The colour quickly drained from Stitchum's face as he sheepishly followed him into the office. I was waiting in the inspector's room wishing I could have been a fly on the wall in there. Obviously Stitchum's plan to get everyone 'off the hook' had backfired in a big way. Although it was absolutely nothing to do with me, I felt guilty for having to expose what was after all a fairly innocent cover up. After about ten minutes, Andrew appeared again and asked me politely if I would come into his office.

"Yes, of course," I replied.

It seemed there was some formal sort of inquest underway.

"I know exactly what's been going on," he said focusing on me. "I'm not having a go at you. Under the circumstances it was decent of you to offer to get them out of a mess." He then paused for a moment to give Stitchum and Soakum an evil sneer. "Mrs Walsh said that you told her there was a problem with the plastering, is that correct?"

"Quite correct," I confirmed.

"What's the problem?"

"To be quite honest, as it's your business, I think you ought to go around there and have a look at it."

He stared at me almost with disbelief that I should dare to address him in this way. Feeling quite angry myself, I continued;

"Had it had been at all possible, I would have fitted the new skirting there. I have always been willing to help any one out of a crisis if I can. The problem is the plastering at that property has been done by a blind gorilla. It really is the worst I have ever seen in my life."

Obviously, totally and utterly flabbergasted: he seemed completely lost for words and we were all, it seemed, spared a flogging. At least: for the moment. I now had a better understanding of why Soakum had taken to the drink. I could also understand why his drinking problem was tolerated. It would have been virtually impossible for them to have found a replacement for him.

Stitchum was not in the best of spirits after this little furore and was even more disheartened by the fact that his first two inspections had turned out to be a waste of time. The one we were going to look at now was according to him a little more promising.

"It's a church," he explained, "strangely enough it's just at the bottom of my road. We've got to somehow get in the roof. I hope the geezer there's got some tall ladders because if I remember rightly it's about sixty foot high."

When we arrived the grey haired obsequious church warden was waiting eagerly outside in the bitterly cold wind with two enormous ladders. We carted them inside where the warden pointed to a large hatch at least sixty feet above the ground. He explained that the ladders did not extend right up to the access hatch but up to some metal rungs that were fixed into the stonework below the hatch. The idea being that the ladders would get us on to the metal rungs which were about forty feet above the ground, we could then climb up the metal rungs another twenty feet or so which would take us to the hatch. I definitely didn't like the sound of this. After a major effort and feat of strength, we managed to get the ladders upright and in position. I explained to Stitchum that I had no real desire to go up there and look in the roof however interesting it might be. I had a strange vision of the rungs coming out of the stonework and of us both descending sixty feet or so rapidly on to the stone flooring below.

"Nothing to it," he stated, "you need to get used to these, we get quite a few of them."

"Alright, you can go first," I advised.

Initially it didn't present much of a problem, but as we got near the top where the rungs were the ladder started whipping, bowing and bending in a rather disconcerting manner. Looking down was definitely not to be advised. Stitchum hauled himself off the top of the ladder on to the first metal rung.

"Come on, it's quite safe," he shouted.

After he'd climbed a further half a dozen rungs, I followed his actions and hauled myself off the ladder on to the metal rungs. A few seconds later I heard him scream "Jesus." I was covered in a cloud of dust and bits of mortar. Seconds later there was a loud metallic clang and ringing sound from below. One of the grab holds or rungs had completely come out of the stonework and fallen down within a few feet of where the church warden was standing.

"Christ mate," Stitchum shouted down to the warden, "you've definitely got God on your side."

"Right that's it," I said, "sod this, I've had enough of this game," I shouted up to him, "I'm going down."

"Come on, don't be a coward," he shouted back, "we're nearly there now."

He was now standing directly underneath a large wooden hatch which was about five feet wide by three feet.

"How does this open?" he bellowed down to the warden.

"It's hinged, you just push it," a disembodied voice wafted back that seemed miles away.

"I can't move it, it's too heavy, it won't budge; if you climb up another couple of feet I can put a foot on your shoulder, and get underneath it."

"I'm not ecstatic about that idea," I told him.

"Nah, come on, it'll be easy mate, we've got this far, it's quite safe."

Reluctantly, I climbed up two more rungs and was directly underneath him. A size twelve policeman's boot placed itself firmly on my shoulder. As he pushed upwards, the boot dug in further. I definitely wasn't enjoying this. I couldn't see what was happening my face was contorted with the pain, but heard a loud creaking, and then a bang, followed by a cloud of dust which covered both of us. He'd opened it. The boot was removed from my shoulder, and after a few grunts and deafening belch, he hauled himself in. I did likewise, realizing that this was a ridiculously dangerous manoeuvre sixty feet above the ground.

"Cracked it," he said triumphantly.

"Yes, I think you have." I replied, feeling my collar bone.

The old oak roof was filthy dirty, everything covered in fine black silt. It was hard to estimate the length of it but it seemed to go on forever.

"Anything up here?" I asked.

"We'll make bloody sure there is; I'm not doing this for nothing. The whole area, all the timbers, everything, all needs to vacuumed out and then all the timbers need spraying with insecticide."

"For what?" I enquired.

"For about twelve hundred quid I reckon," he replied.

After ten minutes or so of crawling around the roof space Stitchum seemed quite agitated and tense. We were both now completely coated with fine black dust.

"Right, we've seen enough, you go down first and I'll follow you. I'll need to put a foot on your shoulder again to close the hatch so wait for me."

"Okay, I confirmed," convinced now that I would end up deformed after this exercise.

I swung myself out of the roof hatch, with both legs swinging in the air trying to find the metal rungs in the wall with my feet. I located one with my right foot; let go of the frame around the hatch and made a flying leap with both arms outstretched and grabbed another rung. I felt enormously relieved; knowing that one minor misjudgement at this height would have been fatal. It was still necessary to climb down the metal rungs in the stonework, and then get on to the ladders, but that was child's play compared with actually getting out of the roof. I waited, hanging on to these metal rungs as instructed for a couple of minutes but there was no sign of the size twelve's dangling out of the hatch.

"Alright?" I shouted up.

There was no response.

"Stitchum, are you coming down? Are you alright?"

"No," he said.

"What's the problem?"

"I can't do it."

65

"What do you mean?"

"It's no good, I can't do it, the 'bottle's' gone."

"Come on, there's nothing to it." I said.

"No, I'm staying up here for a while, I can't breathe properly."

"Do you want me to get some help?" I asked.

"Yeah, call the fire brigade."

"Are you serious?"

"Yeah."

"Hang on, don't worry, I'll go and phone them now."

The warden below couldn't quite understand what was happening; he'd thought that I had come down to get some more equipment.

"How are you chaps getting on up there?" he asked innocently.

"Well, we've finished the inspection, but there is a slight problem. Is there a telephone here in the church?"

"Yes there is a phone in the office. Can I ask what the problem is?" he enquired.

"We need to get the fire brigade," I said.

"Oh my god: you haven't started a fire up there have you?"

"No, it's nothing like that. It's the metal rungs in the stonework, they're loose. It's too dangerous to try and climb out of the roof on to them. I just managed it but my colleague is heavier than me and it's not worth taking the risk."

"Oh dear. Oh dear", he exclaimed, "I will go and telephone them for you, I'm so sorry; I thought they were quite secure."

"Hardly" I replied caustically, "one of them landed a few feet from where you were standing."

As he went off to make the call, I decided I had better go up and fill Stitchum in: knowing that if it got back to the office that he'd had a panic attack in a church roof and was too frightened to get out his life wouldn't be worth living.

Within just a few minutes the church was buzzing with yellow helmeted firemen. A gigantic ladder was brought in, and within minutes they had coaxed Stitchum out of the roof. He actually knew two of the firemen, who both sympathized with his plight...or at least pretended to.

We helped the warden, who appeared to be incredibly stressed by this turn of events to take the ladders down and put them away. We were just leaving when he called us back.

"By the way, I should have asked you only I know the committee will ask me, what's it like up there?"

"Terrible, absolutely terrible," Stitchum replied.

As we both now looked rather like nylon coated chimney sweeps, we drove back to the office to avail ourselves of the washroom facilities before carrying out the fourth and final inspection of the day. Time was pressing on and Stitchum, although now much calmer was fretting about missing the lunch time slot.

"I've got a feeling the next one's going to be a complete waste of time," he said despondently.

"Why's that?" I asked.

"Well it's for 'Maurice the Miser'."

"Who's he?"

"He's a bloke that owns hundreds of properties in the town, all in terrible condition, and all let out at extortionate rents. The only time he does some work on them is when the tenants complain and the local authority serves notices on him. You'll meet him; we've got an appointment for twelve thirty."

No less than fifteen minutes later we were knocking on the door of a scruffy looking basement flat below a large dilapidated tenement building in the centre of the town. The door opened almost immediately and Maurice the Miser appeared. An extremely strange looking fellow: a sort of modern day Shylock. His physiognomy was almost an exact caricature of an old east end Jew. His archetypal hooked nose

67

had dew drops hanging from it which he was constantly removing with the back of his gnarled and bony hand.

"Two of you?" he growled, "It needs two of you already to look at a bit of damp?"

"No" Stitchum said, "Clive is learning the business."

"Business, business, don't talk about business, I never get a moments peace."

"I've got a note here that says you've got a damp problem," Stitchum said.

"Ah it's nothing really, don't start thinking lots of money, I'm a poor man trying to survive on a few shillings. Follow me, I'll show you what they're complaining about."
We followed him along a dark narrow hallway which led into a large bed sitting room. The stench of dampness was almost overpowering .The plaster was literally hanging off the walls and the solid floor was visibly wet.

"Here, this is it, there's a bit of damp over there maybe, nothing serious," he said. "All old properties have got a bit of damp: but do people understand this? Of course they don't. It's a beautiful little flat, so it's got a bit of damp already? They want a palace nowadays for thirty five quid a week?"

Whilst this was going on I was fascinated if not mesmerized by Maurice. He reminded me very much of some sort of theatrical pantomime character. He was a fairly diminutive figure, about five feet four and probably only about seven stone. He had an incredibly deep penetrating voice and seemed completely oblivious of the vile hawking and snorting noises he made after every sentence. One side of his strange shaped head was almost completely bald. To overcome this, the greasy black dandruff coated hair that had sprouted on the other side was brushed over and completely obscured one ear. The other exposed ear stuck out and was disproportionately large to the size of his head. His eyes were really just bloodshot slits being almost completely obscured by the grey baggy lids. Every time he advised us that the damp in the flat was 'nothing', he grinned with self satisfaction revealing some yellow tombstone teeth which had a sizeable gap in the centre which produced a hissing sound to his speech.

"It's not just one area" Stitchum stated disdainfully, "the whole room including the floor is soaking wet: the whole lot, all the plaster, needs completely hacking off: damp proofing and replastering. You're looking at about four grand at least."

"Four grand? Four grand? Don't be silly, where am I supposed to get four grand? A little bit of damp and he wants four grand already?" he said, looking at me. "Which planet have you come from? Listen, I'm a poor man, but I'm a reasonable man: so there's a bit of damp? And you're telling me four grand already? Speak English, we're talking a couple of hundred pounds, I'll have to find it from somewhere, stop talking about four grand it's not even funny."

Realizing the situation was hopeless; Stitchum said he should get other estimates which might be a lot cheaper. Maurice showed us to the door cursing, blaspheming, and muttering 'four grand, four grand, and he wants four grand already'.

"Will you bother to send him an estimate?" I asked when we were back in the car.

Stitchum looked quite amazed at my question.

"What do you think?" he asked belligerently.

"Well I certainly wouldn't have thought so, but with all the rigid rules and regulations you've been telling me about, I wondered if you had to send one out regardless."

"No mate that really would be grasping at straws."

We headed towards the cafe, where on this occasion; Stitchum had a far more leisurely lunch, allowing himself a whole eleven and a half minutes this time to demolish the same amount of food as on the previous day. Needless to say our conversation during the drive back to the office was interspersed by the usual eructation's: notwithstanding the extra time allocated by Stitchum for his urgent feeding frenzy. Back at the office it was unfortunately necessary to hear more of the depressing exploits of the other inspectors: whilst Stitchum drafted out his report and estimate in respect of the church roof which astutely included as the penultimate paragraph a few lines insisting that; 'Should you wish to proceed with the treatments specified; safe access to the roof space must be provided by yourselves prior to our arrival on site'.

The remainder of the afternoon, which seemed to drag, was spent writing out mock reports, studying photographs of various sorts of fungi, and for quite a fair bit of the last hour: wondering what on earth I was doing there in the first place.

The following day it was agreed that I would accompany Cheatum on his inspections as Stitchum had a doctor's appointment and wouldn't be around first thing in the morning. Naturally, I found it immensely difficult to contain my excitement at the prospect of this.

Chapter Five

The odious slimy Cheatum was delighted that due to a miscalculation of traffic conditions I had arrived ten minutes early. I found him seated at one of the battered old desks in the inspector's room smoking an evil smelling cheroot whilst examining the details of the poor unsuspecting victims who we were just about to visit: those naïve innocent people that had somehow allowed themselves to be beguiled by the slick reassuring advertising ploys that Sprayum & Scarper excelled at.

"Allo Clive pleased to see, you're nice and early. We're going to have to fly around a bit today. I've got the usual four to do, plus I've taken two from Stitchum," he drawled in a smarmy sickly sweet voice.

"Go and grab yourself a cup of tea, and while you're at it: I'll av a refill myself, two sugars if you'd be so kind, then we'll work out a plan of action, as it were."

I walked off to the kitchen to carry out this command wondering if I could somehow find an extension to my level of tolerance which was nearing depletion purely at the very sight of this oily repugnant individual.

"Ah thanks Clive, that's really very kind of you, much appreciated."

"What sort of problems have we got to look at today?" I enquired.

"Just about everything, a fine assortment," he drawled, "for us it's a bit like being a spider in a web really. You've got to be patient, and at the same time you've got to know exactly when to strike as it were. Go in too quickly and you'll frighten them off. If you've been running a building company then you are going to know exactly what I mean."

"I know what you mean," I replied, "but to be honest I've never had to employ that sort of cunning. All the work we did was what people actually wanted. Most of the time they knew precisely what it was they wanted to achieve; it wasn't really necessary to sell them anything. The clients we did work for came to us from a recommendation from previous clients, or architects and surveyors." I responded without attempting to conceal my utter contempt for this undisguised snake in the grass.

"Well, lucky you!" He replied obsequiously. "Finished your tea have you? We'd better get this show on the road as it were. I'd better tell you that I work in a slightly different way to the others. They all go hell bent on reaching their twelve grand minimum sales targets and then they rely on the commission they make over that. I make sure I reach the twelve grand as quickly as possible; which you have to of course, otherwise they kick you out, and then I look after the one that matters as it were, myself; if you know what I mean."

"Not really, I'm intrigued."

"Well, let's say I can convince somebody that they need a new floor for example: I'll quote them a figure for doing it, and although I've won them over, as it were, it might be that they can't afford to have it done. This crops up a fair bit because Sprayum & Scarper's prices are not exactly cheap if you know what I mean, particularly when V.A.T. is added. Rather than lose the job to a competitor I point them in the right direction as it were."

"Which direction is that?" I enquired, seriously tempted to add 'as it were'.

"Well let's say I don't let the opposition have it if I can help it."

How?" I asked feeling more than a little irritated that he wouldn't come straight out with whatever devious plan he'd devised.

"Let me explain: if it turns out that I've convinced them they need a new floor and we don't get the job, then what I've done in effect is left them as a nice succulent dish for all the other companies to go round and eat. Now we can't have that can we? I tell them that I know a small builder; a very reputable one you understand that has just had a job held up over some planning problem, and I tell them I feel sure if I spoke to him he would do the job for them at about a third cheaper than the price I had quoted them. They might ask how is it possible he can do this and of course I have the perfect answer: that is: firstly, he is not V.A.T. registered so there's a big saving there, and secondly, he doesn't have the massive overheads of Sprayum & Scarper, so he's not looking for the same profit. There eyes normally light up and then they want his phone number. The beauty of this is that I have a nice little arrangement going with a couple of builders who give me five per cent on anything I aim in their direction. Nice one eh? It's quite an improvement on the two per cent I would have earned from Sprayum & Scarper in the first place."

"Clever," I had to agree.

"There's another little perk that's not to be ignored, particularly for me as I used to be in the double glazing business. A lot of these properties that we look at need new windows and doors. I always ask them if they're thinking about this and explain that I have relatives in the business and can get them a thirty per cent discount if I say that it's for a friend of mine. I pick up another five per cent on these jobs as well from a couple of geezers I know in the game."

"Is there anything you're not 'into'?" I asked him.

"Well, cosmetic surgery would be a really nice one: very profitable operation that one . . . if you forgive the pun. Most of the clients I come across look so glum and down in the

73

mouth; I think it would be a definite winner. Trouble is I don't know any plastic surgeons at this moment in time, but I always keep my eyes and ears open as it were."

The first one we were off to see this morning was a suspected case of dry rot in a bathroom floor. The house was a mid Victorian end of terrace house. The owners, a pleasant middle aged couple, had lived there for many years and were now in the process of having a new bathroom installed. In taking up the old floor tiles in order to lift the floorboards, their plumber had noticed that a couple of the floorboards were rotten under the bath where the waste had been leaking. Evidently he thought it was just wet rot, but wasn't absolutely sure, and advised the owners to get a 'specialist company' to check it out. When Cheatum saw the area in question he advised them that at first glance it did certainly look like dry rot, and that he would need to take further floorboards up and carry out some 'tests'. More boards were lifted in the adjoining bedroom, he poked around under the floor, examined his fingernails, scratched his bottom, and then after about fifteen minutes he suddenly declared that it was 'true dry rot', and thank God the plumber had the good sense to bring their attention to it before it 'ripped' through the whole house. Due to the urgency of the situation an immediate plan was put into action. The owners certainly couldn't continue to live there, not only because their toilet had to come out: but more importantly the spores were harmful, and if breathed in could cause a serious chest infection which was resulted in large pustules rather like buboes forming all over their skin which was often fatal. The owners of this property were now clearly quite terrified. A telephone call to the emergency treatment room at Sprayum & Scarper confirmed that in the light of this grave emergency, two specialist dry rot 'technicians' could start at eight o'clock the next morning. Cheatum explained to the clients that at this stage it would not be possible to let them have an estimate as they had to get to the bottom of it and determine the full extent of the outbreak.

74

This would entail hacking off all the wall plaster in the bathroom, also on the partition wall of the adjoining bedroom, and one metre down from the ceiling in the kitchen. All of the exposed brickwork would have to be sterilized with a powerful fungicide and then the walls replastered. 'Don't worry 'sir' we won't stop until we've uncovered the very last strand of it' he said, almost feigning a lump in his throat at the plight of this poor couple. Without questioning Cheatum's diagnosis, and without further delay, they both began packing suitcases in order to escape these dangerous spores.

"Have you any idea what the total cost will be of getting rid of it?" The owner asked.

"I really can't tell at this stage 'sir, just think in thousands rather than hundreds, is the best I can come up with at this precise moment in time. I'm afraid when we come across something like this, which I must admit isn't that often, we just can't afford to cut corners, even if we wanted to."

"No, I understand," the owner said, "we are so pleased to have found you. What shall we do about letting your men in tomorrow if we are not going to be here?"

"No problem 'sir', if you have a spare set of keys I will be here myself at eight o'clock, I will meet them here. I have to examine the breathing apparatus they wear before they start, and just run through the decontamination details with them. Health and safety is of paramount importance where there is any danger of dry rot spores being released into the atmosphere. I shall then be supervising the work from start to finish. When we come across these unfortunate cases we try to minimize the worry and stress that is engendered by the nature of the treatments required."

"Did you see any dry rot there?" I asked him as we drove off.

"Well, not exactly, but you know, better safe than sorry. We'll talk about that later."

"The next one could be quite interesting," Cheatum declared, now looking more confident and sleazy than ever.

"What is it?" I enquired, now really preparing myself for anything.

"It's a small hotel I reckon. If the description on the inspection sheet here is anything to go by. It's got twelve bedrooms and four reception rooms, plus the owner's accommodation. Evidently it's a remortgage situation. That normally means that the owner is a bit strapped for cash, probably due to having had a quiet season. Very wisely the bank that's offering the new mortgage wants the whole thing checked out for woodworm before releasing the advance. These can be very sweet," he stated in his sickly smarmy drawl.

"What do you mean exactly by 'very sweet'?" I don't quite understand."

"Can you imagine the disruption and inconvenience that would be caused if the whole place; not just the roof, but all the floors as well, all had to be treated for woodworm? It would be a complete bleeding nightmare."

"I'm a little confused," I said, "I do understand what you mean, it would of course be virtually impossible to treat it all while guests were staying there. So why do you say it could be very sweet?"

"Well look at it the way I see it. The owner's got the loan approved; he obviously needs the money, and judging by the look of him; probably quite urgently. The bank won't release the cheque to him until he's had the whole building checked out for woodworm. If there's woodworm there which you and I both know there will be: he's got no choice other than to empty the hotel of all the guests, clear all the rooms out, take up all the carpets and floor coverings etc, It would take a week to treat it: another week for the floors to dry, and probably another week to have all the carpets re-laid and all the furniture put back. Do you understand where I'm coming from yet?"

"I've got a rough idea," I replied.

"The vital thing that we have to do is find some worm holes in one of the bedrooms. The roof of course would be a bonus but I'm not that interested in that at the moment. Once we've found it in the bedrooms, I can sit down and have a nice little chat with him on exactly how I help him out of his obvious dilemma. Faced with the sort of problems there could be: what he's going to want more than anything, is a letter from a reputable 'specialist company' saying something to the effect that they've carried out a detailed inspection of all parts of the property and were unable to find any evidence of woodworm. Just think that would get him completely off the hook. He'd get his money in a few days. No complications whatsoever. Now what do you think a letter like that would be worth to him? If you work it out even roughly the cost of the rooms being vacant for two or three weeks, the cost of the treatments, and then add on taking out the furnishings, the carpets and everything else: and then . . . putting it all back again. He certainly wouldn't see any change out of five grand. On that simple little calculation I would estimate that such a letter must be an absolute bargain at five hundred quid. In these situations I see myself being what you might call a loss adjuster as it were."

Cheatum could hardly contain his joy in seeing the hotel car park was almost full of cars as we turned into the driveway.

"Don't say anything," he instructed, "look, listen and learn!"

We announced our presence at the little reception area and waited for Mr Brown the owner to arrive. A few minutes later a chubby middle aged jovial chap appeared with bright eyes and a red unhealthy looking complexion.

"Ah you're from Sprayum & Scarper," he stated. "Good of you to be so punctual. The position is I'm remortgaging the hotel and my bank just wants the property checked for woodworm. I can't think why they've come up with this: I had the whole property looked at five years ago and there

77

wasn't a sign of woodworm anywhere. I suppose they're just protecting they're interests you know what bank's are like these days."

"Yes indeed sir," Cheatum concurred. "May I suggest we inspect the roof first 'sir' then we will need to look at all the bedrooms."

"The roof won't present any problems. The bedrooms could be a little more difficult: some of them will be free and others will still be occupied. If you would be good enough to do the roof first and then go down to reception, our young lady will let you know which rooms are vacant and will let you have the keys to these."

"Yes indeed 'sir', Cheatum replied. "We do understand that these inspections can be a little 'intrusive' as it were and we shall make every endeavour to do what we have to do as painlessly as possible."

Once we were both inside the roof the creepy sinister grin returned to Cheatum's face.

"You really can't miss it up here," he confirmed, before we'd had a chance to examine any of the timbers. After searching around for about twenty minutes we did eventually find some old flight holes which Cheatum immediately declared was in fact an active scattered infestation of woodworm. Five of the bedrooms were unoccupied. After pulling up corners of the fitted carpets, it became apparent that as part of the fire regulations all the bedroom floors had been covered in hardboard. This made access to the floorboards virtually impossible without ripping up large sections of it. Cheatum was now like a man possessed. It didn't matter to him now what was involved; he was quite determined to find some flight holes even if it meant tearing the whole building apart. The next extreme measure was to remove the bath panels from the en suite bathrooms. Being plastic, he was able to do this without too much difficulty, although one did split where he had yanked it off as his fury and desperation increased. Under the bath of the third one he found exactly what he was looking for. Although, very old, there were a few flight holes in one of the floorboards.

"Oh dear," Cheatum sighed, "Such a shame, I thought for a moment Mr Brown was going to be lucky. We'd better go and tell him what we've found so that he can see for himself," he drawled in his smarmy servile voice.

A few moments later, all that could be seen of Mr Brown, were his ample posteriors poking out from under the bath. Crawling out, even redder in the face than before, and now with a cobweb hanging from his ear he asked Cheatum if it was possible just to spray this small area under the bath.

Any hope of this was quickly dispelled, as it was explained to Mr Brown that if there was woodworm here it would certainly be in the floorboards and joists of the rest of the building. Unfortunately our inspection had also revealed evidence of it in the roof, and the whole property now quite definitely needed woodworm eradication treatment.

"Right 'sir' Cheatum almost whispered as if trying to show a compassionate side to his vile nature.

"I've worked out some figures for you, is there somewhere we can go to discuss the best possible way to deal with this problem?"

I was instructed to replace the bath panel, and take the tools down to the car whilst this discussion took place. After about twenty minutes Cheatum appeared, looking buoyant.

"All went according to plan," he stated. "I always think it's most satisfying when you can solve people's problems so quickly and painlessly. I think that's what's called job satisfaction."

"Would it not have been possible for him to have got other specialist companies in?" I asked him. "I would have thought that one of them would have explained that there wasn't any woodworm there and simply written a letter to confirm it. Perhaps charge a small amount for the visit and administration?"

"You wouldn't find a company like that in this town mate: if anyone operated like that they wouldn't stay in business very long. Everyone in this game has got to make damn sure they get the maximum out of every enquiry."

Although appearing, or more accurately, wanting to appear relaxed and 'laid back', the impression he undoubtedly wished to convey with his servile unctuous façade: Cheatum was in fact quite remarkably bigoted and narrow minded. The long list of people he hated and despised included in his words, 'darkies', ' kikes', 'chinkies', 'taffies', 'micks', 'dykes' and 'shirt lifters' to name just a few. I asked him what he meant by 'darkies', and was told it encompassed anyone no matter where they came from that had a dark skin. For him they were all 'niggers' and 'spades', and should 'bugger off' back to their own country. His main objection to this section of the community was that they were lazy and dishonest and simply couldn't be trusted. Not just a few of them he emphasized, but all of them without exception. Other people he loathed included teachers, the police, members of the clergy, politicians, (especially Margaret Thatcher), who he had seriously thought about 'bumping off' and probably most of all social workers. The more time I spent listening to Cheatum, the more I realized that he was in fact quite seriously mentally deranged. I asked him how he was able to accept that Stitchum was an ex policeman and how it was possible that he could cope with this. 'Well he's a reformed character now' was his response; presumably eluding to the fact that he was now as crooked and dishonest as the rest of them.

Having spent more time than was anticipated at the hotel we were now running late and would only be able to fit one more inspection in before lunch. This was for a builder who was in the process of constructing a room in the roof. He'd noticed some woodworm holes in the ceiling joists and rafters and thought it would be wise for the client to have the timbers treated before they were all encased in plasterboard and new flooring. Cheatum was not exactly buoyant about this enquiry as even with his specially honed skills and animal cunning, he knew it would be impossible to secure anything other than a fair price for the work. He tried to convince the builder that if there was woodworm in the roof, it would almost certainly be present in the rest of the house. The builder, a taciturn, dull man with an obvious dislike of house inspectors was clearly irritated by Cheatum's attempt to find more work. This resulted in our making a hasty retreat after only having been at the property for five minutes with an order to spray the roof timbers, and a builder now convinced that woodworm was not so much of a problem as the high pressure salesmen employed by the various companies.

Cheatum's lunch venue was a mobile roadside burger stall. According to Cheatum, the fellow who owned it was a decent geezer that had 'had a bit of bother' and now found it difficult obtaining any other form of employment.

"What do you mean by 'a bit of bother'?" I enquired.

"Well, he's been out of circulation as it were for the last eight years."

"Where's he been?"

"One of her majesty's holiday camps," he sniggered.

"Why? What did he do?"

"What it was, he and his partner used to run a car sales site, not that far from here actually. I used to work for them flogging motors. One evening after I'd left, they had an argument over money and Brian, the geezer with the burger van lost his rag and stoved the other guy's head in with a wheel brace. The jury accepted that he didn't intend to kill him and accepted that it was just done in a fit of temper and not premeditated as it were.

"Best not complain to him about the burgers them?"

"Nah, don't worry about Brian, he's a pussy cat. We're all entitled to get a little aerated now and then with things that annoy us," he stated as we advanced towards the van with more than just a little trepidation on my part.

Brian, it seemed was still in 'the motor trade', having lost his business after the unfortunate debacle with his partner. He was now reduced to buying old cars at auctions, 'spivving' them up as he called it and selling them on from home purporting it to be a private sale. Business at the burger stall wasn't exactly brisk but this supplemented his meagre income. He explained to Cheatum that he was trying to find a new business partner that would be prepared to invest some money in a 'decent site' somewhere, but for some inexplicable reason was having difficulty in attracting a suitable investor. It now became clear that another of Cheatum's activities included selling the odd car for him from home with Cheatum posing as a private seller. For this he received ten per cent commission, or fifty per cent in excess of the sale price stated by Brian. Extraordinarily, the arrangement seemed to work satisfactorily for both of them.

Lunch times were not exactly the highlight of the day, but in comparison with sitting in the hot stuffy greasy spoon with Stitchum: Standing outside this burger van in the freezing cold grasping a polystyrene cup of coffee tasting like battery acid and a greasy hamburger of dubious origin was infinitely preferable.

Our next inspection was referred to as a 'remedial', which meant this was a possible claim under guarantee. The work in question, a new chemical damp proof course and what was euphemistically described as replastering, had been carried out about two years ago, and the owner was now complaining that the work had failed. It was the policy with Sprayum & Scarper to charge a reinspection fee of one hundred pounds to examine this. If upon inspection it was considered by one of their 'technical experts' that the claim was valid: any remedial work found necessary would be carried out free of charge under the terms of the guarantee and the inspection fee refunded. Needless to say in practice this rarely occurred. This was possibly aided by the fact that the 'technical expert' received twenty five pounds of the sum paid if he could persuade the victim that the problem, whatever it might have been, was attributable to causes other than any failure of the work carried out by Sprayum & Scarper. The inspectors found no boundaries in their highly imaginative and creative thinking in coming up with good justifiable reasons as to why the damp problem, woodworm or dry rot had returned.

The property we arrived at was no exception. A turn of the century terraced house with large areas of new wet plaster around the ground floor bay window. The owners hadn't redecorated after the company's visit over two years ago as the plaster had remained wet throughout this period. They were advised by a builder they had in to carry out other works that this should have dried out completely six to nine months afterwards, and that there must be a problem with the damp proofing. After carrying out a few 'tests', Cheatum came up with the answer: it was condensation. The owners of the property were not entirely convinced, but had little alternative but to accept his diagnosis, and act on his professional advice in that they should go out and buy a dehumidifier which would solve the problem. According to Cheatum, and his expert assessment of the situation, the people who owned the property only had themselves to blame for being inconsiderate enough to live in the house and thereby creating too much moisture. It does in fact seem quite ludicrous to any rational sane person that the fault or defect in these situations is always inspected by the original company who are not exactly impartial and will go to any lengths to avoid having to do the work again free of charge. Human nature is such that people in any situation are loathe to accept liability for their failures, particularly so when any admission is going to hit them where it hurts. Many people in this position, being unhappy with the fact that they've paid out thousands of pounds and still have the same problem, would contact other specialist companies in the hope that they would inspect the work and find the real reason for the dampness returning. These people quickly discovered that other companies simply weren't interested, knowing the property had already been treated. There would have been little point in their being drawn into a highly contentious situation with a competitor, where there would be nothing in it for them in the end other than having to waste valuable time assisting the victim to obtain some form of resolution. So as a matter of principle they would not retreat anything that was under guarantee by another company, or for that matter even look at it. Chartered surveyors generally, have little or no understanding of chemical damp courses and how they should work, which sort of plaster and admixes are appropriate for a particular type of construction, and so on; which meant that the client had little choice other than to trust the findings of the inspector for the company that installed the thing in the first place. Thankfully now, there are a number of respected and properly qualified remedial treatment consultants who are totally independent, and will if need be, carry out proper on site investigations which often includes analysing brick, and plaster samples, humidity testing, and a whole range of procedures to determine definitively the cause of failure. Needless to say these individuals are not always the best friends of the cowboy treatment companies.

Chapter Six

The next inspection awaiting Cheatum's expertise was a 'key job'; a repossession. The property; an elegant spacious Edwardian semi, had been lavishly fitted out with hand made antique pine kitchen units, marble worktops and numerous other expensive fixtures and fittings, all of which had been vandalised. The marble work tops had been smashed, the doors on the units had been either ripped off, or kicked in and what appeared to be paint stripper had been poured over the built in appliances. The bathroom, which sported a large corner bath with Jacuzzi, twin wash hand basins, a bidet and an expensive glass shower unit had been violently attacked with possibly an axe or a sledge hammer. I assumed that vandals must have broken into the house in some kind of drug induced rampage. According to Cheatum this was not the case at all. Evidently the owners had just before the bailiff's arrival at the property, realized all was lost, and preferred to destroy everything they could in order to prevent anyone else, particularly their building society from benefiting from their efforts.

"Very sad to see this," Cheatum said, trying to sound sincere. "Perhaps they should have thought more about making the mortgage repayments rather than spending thousands of pounds on all this designer rubbish."

Without knowing anything whatsoever about the unfortunate owners, or probably ex owners, he then issued a malignant and totally unjustified tirade on what he called yuppies and the nouveau riche. Evidently, according to him, the owners of this property would have been the sort of people that would 'ponce' around, wearing expensive designer sunglasses, drove a flashy sports car, and used to sit around with their 'fancy' friends, drinking pina colada's and calling each other 'dharling'.

"Yeah, I know their type," he said sneeringly, "all fur coat and no knickers. Alright, let's set to work and see what we can find, there's got to be plenty here. The sort of 'nobs' that owned this were only interested in what showed; underneath all the glitz and glamour we're going to find all sorts of nasty expensive problems," he confirmed. He then knelt down on the kitchen floor, prized a screwdriver under the laminate flooring, and ripped up a section of it causing a large split in the surface. Driven by his hatred for the owners, he then levered up another piece, splitting this section in half. In an angry frenzy he continued until a large area of the expensive laminate flooring had been desecrated. Floorboards were then lifted with two of them snapping in the middle. Having now gained access to the floor joists, he confirmed the whole property was alive with woodworm. Out of interest, I asked him to show me what he had found. The sinister self satisfied grin returned and now wheezing and out of breath, he pointed to some flight holes that must have been nearly as old as the house.

"There we are: I told you we'd find it."

"True, but they're old holes, there's no sign of anything active is there." I said.

"Ah, you can never be too sure, always err on the safe side. Just think what a terrible thing it would be if another lot of nice young yuppies move in only to find that they've got woodworm and that the dozy house inspector that looked at the property for them failed to spot it. I tell you what mate whether it's active or not, they'd sue the bleeding arse off you, that's the way these yuppies behave."

As would be expected, a quick check confirmed that readings from a moisture meter confirmed beyond doubt that the whole property was wringing wet and now needed a new damp proof course. When I asked Cheatum to show me where he got these readings from he pointed to the threshold under the back door of the kitchen where rainwater had been seeping through a crack under the cill. Our inspection of the property was concluded after a quick search in the wardrobes and vanity units to see if any jewellery or other valuables might have been left behind by the departing 'yuppies'. The fact that they had been inconsiderate enough not to have left something of value annoyed Cheatum even more.

Our final inspection of the day was a 1960s bungalow, all in an immaculate condition. The owner, an elderly widow, had been searching around the loft for items to contribute to a local jumble sale and had noticed some woodworm holes around the loft hatch. Unlike most of the victims that called in Sprayum & Scarper, she was aware that having flight holes in timber didn't necessarily mean that the beetle was still there; she really just wanted peace of mind, and for 'a specialist company' to confirm that these were really just old flight holes and nothing to worry about. However, unsurprisingly, Cheatum was not of the same opinion. After a cursory look at the roof timbers, he advised her mournfully that the beetle was still very much there, and that as a matter of urgency, the roof timbers must be treated. The elderly woman was still more than a little sceptical and required some convincing.

"It's not hard to see them up there." Cheatum stated with an air of certainty, "here, look, I've brought some down for you to see."

He then produced a small plastic specimen pot from the pocket of his grubby nylon overall and handed it to her. Inside were some tiny dead insects, possibly beetles or bugs of some kind: it didn't really matter. It did the trick and the usual routine followed: A quick telephone call to the emergency treatment room alerted Soakum to this catastrophe. This ensured that the treatments were programmed as a matter of the utmost urgency before the roof timbers were weakened to such an extent by this 'horrible' infestation that the whole roof collapses.

As that was the last victim of the day we headed back to the office to start on the report writing. Cheatum's first consideration was to draft out the letter he'd agreed to write to Mr Brown at the hotel. He wrote out a few lines on a piece of paper and took this straight to the typing pool and waited for it, hovering over the young typist with a sickly grovelling grin on his face. He then slouched into the work planning room to tie up the final details with Soakum for the 'dry rot' job that was to commence in the morning.   Whilst he drafted out his reports I chatted with the others who were interested to know how many 'hits' we'd had. Robbum wasn't in the best of spirits, evidently he'd wasted nearly two hours trying to convince a local doctor that he had a nasty outbreak of dry rot, but without success, and another hour failing to convince a young couple that the basement flat they had just bought was so damp that it presented a serious health risk and that they should vacate it immediately. He'd managed to secure two small jobs that were described by him as 'tiddlers'.

"It gets harder and harder every day this business," Robbum moaned, "half the trouble is that now, there are a lot of villains out there and people don't know who to trust."

"That's quite true," Trickum agreed, the problem is that a lot of the 'inspectors' that are employed by other companies haven't had any proper training, they're not what you might call 'professional' like us, and some of them are just simply dishonest."

Stitchum was talking to a possible victim on the telephone, and was clearly becoming irritated with this chatter going on in the background;

"Well sir, it's obviously not for me to tell you what to do but I think you would be very unwise indeed to cancel the job.

I hate to say so sir, but I can imagine the damage that dry rot will cause to all that beautiful panelling and the cost of eradicating it and then reinstating everything would be astronomical. No sir, no, I'm not saying that Squirt and Leggit don't know what their talking about, I just know that in this instance they have got it wrong. All right sir, you've made a sensible decision, thank you sir ...Goodbye."

"YES!" he shouted manically, "YES! Bastards, they tried it on and it failed." That was the judge," he said, looking at me. "Just after we'd left, some 'chancer' from Squirt's lot called round there and told him the musty smell was caused by condensation. Tried to flog him two dehumidifiers they did at five hundred quid each and damn nearly got away with it. It only goes to prove what I just heard Trickum saying a few minutes ago: you really can't trust anyone these days."

Without wishing to embarrass Cheatum after his little deal with the hotel owner, I asked them all if they ever accepted that many of the flight holes they inspected were without doubt very old, and that it was patently obvious that the beetle had long since flown off: and that spraying timbers in these situations was completely and utterly pointless. Did they ever explain this to the victim? The answer that they all came up with was unanimous. Apart from the most obvious money consideration, they all agreed that if they were paid a proper basic wage without any commission, it would still not be possible to do this. Interestingly; the reason was that if they were to do this, and confirm it in writing, they would leave both themselves and the company in a situation where they were likely to be the subject of claims and legal proceedings.

"It's basically because of all the sharks and villains out there," Trickum explained. If we were to do that and the punter then gets two or three other reports: the other reports are all going to say that there is an active infestation of woodworm there. Then we have to spend hours trying to convince them that this is not the case. This is a fact. The danger lies where the punter has called us in just before they bought the house, and afterwards gets other firms round to give another opinion. This often happens when they move in and start doing work on the property. It's often a plumber, electrician, or carpet fitter; people that profess to be experts on every bleeding thing that spot the flight holes. Old, yes they probably are in most cases; but this sows the seeds of doubt in the owner's minds and casts doubt on Sprayum & Scarper's findings. They then get three or four other companies to look at it who will all say the woodworm is active and send their estimates in for treating it. They then phone us, and ask us how is it three other 'specialist' firms have all confirmed that the woodworm is active and needs eradicating. The next thing you get is a solicitor's letter accusing you of negligence together with a claim for damages. In a way it would be nice if everyone was honest and everyone played by the rules, but sadly this isn't the case."

"But if this were so, you probably wouldn't have a job, and Sprayum & Scarper would be forced to either close up, or seriously reduce the size of their operation wouldn't they?"

"Exactly," Trickum agreed, "so why argue and criticize the present state of affairs?"

"What about rising damp and dry rot then?" I asked.

"That's slightly different," Trickum explained, "It's easier to prove that rising damp exists, but again it's all to do with a more subjective opinion and how you put your case to the client, and of course how you go about selling the treatments. For example; if you find rising damp in one wall of a property, do you quote to treat just that wall? Or do you explain that because the existing damp course has broken down in that wall, it will have disintegrated in other places, and soon the whole property will be like a swimming pool. It is both in the customer's interests and ours to convince them that it would be expensive and pointless just treating one wall when the whole property needs a new damp course. The problem is that there isn't an accepted format to follow.

90

That's why we're continually having punters phone in saying they've had half a dozen reports in respect of a damp problem, and each one is different, with prices ranging from a few hundred to several thousand pounds. There's also the business of replastering. Some firms will say the plaster has to come off, normally a metre high: and others will say that this is not necessary, depending on whether they want to do the plastering or not."

"What about dry rot and wet rot then?" I asked him.

"It's another highly contentious area," he said thoughtfully; "for a start a lot of people employed by 'specialist' firms don't actually know the difference. The ones that do, are always tempted to suggest it's dry rot rather than wet rot, because firstly: dry rot terrifies the life out of people: and secondly the work involved in eradicating it is far more extensive and costly than wet rot where you just cut out and replace the timber that's been affected. The other problem is similar to the diagnosis of woodworm really. If you tell someone that they have wet rot in a timber floor, and that the floor needs replacing, and three other companies all suggest that it's actually dry rot; who is the client going to believe? What the industry needs is education and proper training for its workforce, and serious controls and regulation in respect of reports that are presented to clients, and some form of effective punitive procedure to deter the cowboys: and this mate is never going to happen."

"Sounds like a fairly depressing and hopeless situation to me," I couldn't help remarking.

"Not really," Trickum said," you really have to be philosophical about these things. I always remember the alcoholic's serenity prayer that goes something like;

God grant me the serenity to accept the things I cannot change.
Courage, to change the things that I can
and wisdom to know the difference.

"That's very profound indeed. Were you an alcoholic at some point then?"

"I do beg your pardon," he said with a wry smile, "I'm not a *'has been'*, I still am."

"What caused that do you think?" I asked.

"Probably selling woodworm treatments," he replied laconically.

The prospect of spending the following day with the dour and humourless Stitchum was almost a delight after discovering the hidden charms of the detestable unwholesome Cheatum. By comparison, Stitchum seemed like a virtuous innocent child. After having spent the past two days in this claustrophobic den of petty grasping narrow minded villains, I was seriously beginning to wonder if I would last the first week. TM was evidently impressed with my progress, and more particularly the fact that I had now learned the Latin names of the beetles, the names of the various forms of rot, and the price structure. I found this surprising as none of this was exactly intellectually challenging. He suggested that if I were to continue at this rate, two weeks would probably be a sufficient amount of time for the initial training bearing in mind my previous building experience. Undoubtedly, the pressing need to have a competent house inspector at their Brighton office influenced his decision somewhat. For me it also meant that it might just be possible with a degree of mental effort and determination to last a further seven days in this loathsome environment. The prospect of travelling five hours a day for the next five weeks or so wasn't a pleasant thought either, so perhaps there could be some light at the end of the tunnel.

Driving back to Brighton in the pouring rain I began reflecting on what I perceived as the corruption of commerce generally. The very word 'business', and the even more offensive term *'being in business'* was to my mind loathsome in the extreme. The banks; obviously came high on my list of these greedy grasping parasitical institutions; insurance companies and financial services were definitely second; with estate agents undoubtedly ranking third. The next group really encompassed all the service industries who were really fleas on the back of the housing market. This particular group included woodworm and damp proofing companies, double glazing firms, kitchen companies, and a whole range of *'specialist'* interior design and house makeover firms sprouting up all over the place, whose speciality was actually nothing tangible you could put your finger on; their main *raison d'etre* was to rip you off as quick as they possibly could. If anyone had a skill, a trade or a profession that they'd trained for, or studied for; I believed that they should be adequately recompensed for whatever use this was to people in the market. That's it, I thought; that's exactly it; the thing that annoyed me, and had always done so, were the largely unqualified, often poorly educated mass of the populace that masqueraded as pseudo professional people who were placed in positions by the commercial racketeers to exploit the naïve victims who they came into contact with. Without doubt the most offensive example of this were the spotty nineteen year olds in expensive trendy suits calling themselves *'sales consultants'* or *'sales executives'* that in truth had not yet completely mastered the technique of wiping their own bottoms. Examples of these could be found virtually everywhere. As much as I tried to avoid having any contact with this reviled species; during the course of building extensions and additions to peoples houses, they often appeared unannounced, on the clients instructions to carry out a number of questionable assessments. What intrigued me more than any of these odorous specimens, were the 'feng shui' consultants. As the driving rain pounded against the windscreen, and the dazzle of oncoming headlights caused me to slow down to a snails pace; I was thinking about one of the last building extensions I was working on which was literally a few hours away from being completed, when the 'feng shui expert': a haggard looking flower power throwback from the sixties, wearing sandals, a tatty looking kaftan and numerous rows of beads appeared. Evidently she had been employed by the owner's vacuous wife. Following a quick look round, she declared that the 'chi' was not in balance and that certain things would have to be changed. Not really understanding anything about it, I asked her what she meant. After some strange jargon and then a further spiritual evaluation which entailed her leaning backwards and having what appeared to be a three minute orgasm; she advised me that the windows needed to be changed and the Velux's in the roof were in the wrong positions. I was mildly amused by this until the client asked me what it would cost for me to make these alterations. I later discovered that her sixty minute visit to the property was the equivalent of three days wages for a decent bricklayer. The problem I suppose is that people who are susceptible to this mystical hocus-pocus will always be haunted with fear and insecurity if the advice they were given wasn't strictly adhered to; particularly if then, things start going wrong with their lives.

As I reflected further upon the groups and classes of people that annoyed me; I couldn't help thinking that only a few hours earlier I had been castigating Cheatum's narrow minded bigotry: his endless ranting about the people he hated and despised; and was now beginning to suspect that I had a far more bitter and jaundiced perception of the human race than he did.

The rain was now torrential; even at full speed the wipers couldn't cope. For the past twenty minutes I been crawling along in a convoy just mesmerized by the brake lights of the car in front. Suddenly I saw brightly lighted a pub sign swinging by the roadside and without thinking I turned into the gravel driveway of the pub. I switched the engine off and just sat there for a few moments relieved to no longer hear the monotonous scraping of the wiper blades, and the fan whirring away at full speed trying to keep the windows from misting up. I hadn't made a conscious decision to pull in here and was slightly bemused as to the reason why I had done so. Perhaps what was left of my poor atrophied brain needed a respite from the difficult driving conditions, and was also probably becoming exhausted having to cope with my continual cruel evaluation of the human race.

I was about to start the car again and thought better of it. Might as well go in, have a drink, I thought, and maybe in half an hour or so the rain might have eased off. The pub was completely empty; I sat at the bar and ordered a pint; exchanged the usual pleasantries with the barmaid and then stared into oblivion. Waves of hopelessness and utter despondency were beginning to affect me. Despite trying to keep up some sort of optimistic front, the obvious futility of the course of action I had embarked upon was inescapable. I kept turning over in my mind my reasons for being where I was and doing what I was doing. None of it made any sense. Even if I were to last another week in this loathsome occupation, I knew sooner or later the bank would force a sale on my house and I would be homeless. What was there to be optimistic about? In order to prevent this I would have to totally abandon any principles I had and somehow morph overnight into some kind of super salesman; the very epitome of the kind of person I hated and despised; and then somehow consistently sell at least twice as many 'treatments' than any of the other inspectors in order just to earn enough to survive and slowly pay the bank off; simply to stay in my house. I had already calculated that even if I were able to do this, it would take something like ten years. 'I think I'd rather spend the next ten years inside', I thought, as I sat there with my pint untouched. I became angrier at the injustice of the whole thing. I had always worked hard and never been in debt; had Grimshaw not have panicked I could have kept my building business and paid off the overdraft over a period of time doing something that I enjoyed which provided a valuable service to the community. 'Bastards' I muttered to myself, 'bastards that's what they are'. 'Are you alright luv?' I heard a concerned voice say a couple of times: I had been miles away; I looked up and saw the barmaid in front of me with a frightened expression on her face. 'Anything I can get you sir?' she said nervously: 'no', I replied, 'not unless you have a secret plan to exterminate bank managers'. Realising that the murderous expression that must have been on my face had terrified the life out of her; I got up and left leaving my pint untouched on the bar.

At least the rain had now stopped and the traffic seemed to have eased off a little. I stopped at the off licence on the corner of my road, bought a litre bottle of white wine; a much needed anaesthetic for the nightly ritual of opening the post. Nowadays most of the letters followed a similar vein; from being mildly intimidating to seriously threatening various forms of action that would follow should I be unwise enough to ignore this last and final request etc, etc. I'd heard nothing from Grimshaw since I received the statutory demand from the bank a few days ago. It certainly was extremely difficult trying to live a normal existence in this situation. Trying to sleep at night had become an increasing problem. I often wondered if bank managers were able to sleep soundly after the misery and suffering they were causing their customers.

Chapter Seven

Somehow or other I managed to survive what had now been reduced to a two week training course. For some reason, possibly the fact that they desperately needed an inspector at their Brighton branch I didn't have to undergo their examination. Not that I would have minded. What there was to learn about this wretched business could quite easily be assimilated in a few days.

When I arrived at the Brighton office I was surprised at how small it was: two rooms above a pet shop with a tiny kitchen and a toilet. I was greeted by the manager; a short stocky fellow in a pin striped suit called Felix Chalmers. For some reason I took an instant dislike to him. It annoyed me that I couldn't put my finger on why this was; although thinking about it, anyone called Felix couldn't possibly be likeable; it's a cat's name after all. He did also have an extremely patronising attitude. I felt very much like a traitor knowing that despite his over confident persona, he was about to be 'goonered'. I knew this but he didn't. That didn't seem right to me.

It was now seven thirty in the morning. Felix made some coffee and explained that his inspector 'Connum' would be arriving shortly. The operatives were due in at eight o'clock.

Within the space of ten minutes Felix had divulged his life's history. Evidently before joining Sprayum and Scarper two years ago he was a regional manager for their largest rival 'Killemall'. According to him he was head hunted by

Sprayum and Scarper and offered a substantial sum as a 'golden hello'. I was in no doubt that he had a very fertile imagination and was clearly suffering from delusions of grandeur.

A few moments later, Connum's arrival was preceded by strong alcohol fumes permeating the staircase leading up to where we were standing.

"Morning all," he shouted up the staircase.

"Good morning Connum," Felix said, "this is Clive; he's going to be joining us as from today which will hopefully take the pressure off us a bit."

Connum was about six feet tall, about forty and as thin as a bean pole. His face was haggard; the bloodshot eyes were painful to look at. The fingers on both of his hands were dark brown from nicotine, his breath stank and he had the shakes.

"Nice to meet you," he declared. "Have you been in this business long?"

"Yes, two weeks," I replied.

"Oh don't worry you'll get used to it. The first ten years are the worst, aren't they Felix?"

"No, it's a piece of cake," Felix stated glibly, "once you've got the first fifty inspections or so under your belt the whole thing becomes second nature. It's like falling off a log."

Connum left us with the fumes of his breakfast and went into the kitchen to make himself a coffee. He reappeared a few moments later clad in one of the voluminous blue nylon overalls, holding a chipped mug of coffee vibrating in his brown fingers. His overalls had a rip across the seat, cigarette burns in the arms and paint splatters covering the front of them. Felix asked him if he'd got a clean pair to change into.

"Nah, these are fine," he replied. "If you turn up to do an inspection with immaculate newly ironed overalls the punters lose faith in you immediately. If it looks as though you've actually been doing some work it tends to make them feel more trusting and relaxed."

I immediately warmed towards Connum. He looked fairly harmless to me, and was I thought just another of life's casualties. I wanted to tell him that he was about to be 'goonered' as well but couldn't; Not right now anyway.

After a short while the rest of the ensemble arrived, sounding like a herd of Indian elephants mounting the staircase. The first to appear was Daphne. Daphne was an extremely unattractive woman of indeterminate age; white faced, short mousy hair and completely shapeless. No chance of being distracted here by her seductive feminine charms I thought.

Behind her were the operatives. Collectively they released a most unpleasant odour. There were four of them; presenting quite a disturbing spectacle as they huddled together. When they were introduced to me I found it immensely hard to keep a straight face. They could all have walked off a gothic horror set. The first one, Brian: was about forty, unwashed and unshaven, and wearing an old blue 'Unigate' milkman's jacket with red lapels and the companies' logo displayed on the breast pocket. Below that were threadbare grey track suit bottoms with gaping splits in the knees. On his feet was pair of holey plimsolls.

The second one, Jim: was a bit younger, perhaps mid thirties. Again he was seedy looking, unshaven and had obviously just crawled out of bed. The old dark green sweatshirt he was wearing had the residue of several dinners stuck to the front of it including what appeared to be a not insubstantial amount of chicken tikka masala. To accompany this there were streaks of engine oil and paint splatters. His new blue jeans were several sizes too large with the crotch hanging somewhere around his knees and folds of fabric around his ankles. His feet were encased in a giant pair of black boots. This one had the most fearsome cough I have ever heard, rather like a vicious dog barking.

Operative number three, a man called Doug, was Neanderthal. Hard to tell his age, but I would have thought probably about sixty years old. His long black greasy hair was tied in a pony tail. For some reason he kept shuffling around trying desperately to avoid eye contact with anyone. He was wearing a long ripped black leather coat, striped pyjama bottoms, no socks and old stained carpet slippers.

Buster, the fourth man was quite overweight. I'd guess his age at about fifty. He was clean shaven, bald and looked dangerous. His face was totally expressionless. He was dressed in an old shiny black suit: the trousers of which were held up with several neck ties knotted together, and was wearing a pair of enormous green Wellington boots.

Good God, I thought, if this motley crew are the highly trained workforce that Sprayum and Scarper advertise there might *just* be the odd problem or two at this office. Realising now what was in store for me, I desperately wanted to throw the towel in. I knew I would at some point; it was just a case of when. I kept telling myself that at the moment although I had lost my business, I was at least employed. The poor sods that had worked for me were all still unemployed and could remain so for God knows how long. Every evening I used to buy a newspaper on the way home and scour it for carpentry jobs: but every time I looked through it there was nothing. I couldn't help wondering when Felix and Connum went; what would happen then? Was I supposed to run this ridiculous enterprise on my own? Or would some other poor unfortunate be sent in to help me reorganise what was in effect a complete farce.

Felix gingerly explained to the operative's that only two of them had work to do today as things were pretty quiet at the moment. They drew lots amongst themselves to see who the lucky ones were going to be. In truth none of them wanted to work; they were being paid anyway and there wasn't really much incentive. The two unlucky ones grabbed their job sheets, muttered various expletives and walked back down the stairs to their vehicles. The other two it seemed had a private decorating job and were bickering as to which of them should

100

go and pick up the materials. In the end, they weren't able to agree and left the office arguing and threatening each other.

"They're a good bunch of lads," Felix said unconvincingly. "The problem is trying to find enough work for them, particularly at the moment."

"Yes of course," I said, "It must be difficult."

"Right, let's see if we can get some work in," Connum stated positively as he picked up his inspection sheets for the day. "What's happening Felix? Is Clive coming out with me? Or is he staying here with you?"

"I think it would probably be a good idea if you spend the day here in the office with me," Felix said looking at me, "we can run through the various procedures, and I can explain how everything works."

"Yeah, that sounds good," I said endeavouring to sound interested.

Daphne, who at this point was carrying out a close examination of her tonsils with the mirror of a powder compact, was instructed to make further mugs of coffee whilst Felix and I retired to his office.

"Well, how did you get on down in Southampton?" he asked.

"Fine," I said, preparing myself for whatever was going to come next.

"The problem is that they think that because their operation down there has been so successful that it must work anywhere. I've tried and tried to tell them that this is a totally different area. The people here are more sophisticated, more discerning and generally speaking they're more difficult to win over."

"That's interesting," I said, being completely unable to grasp his reasoning. "Isn't it all about being able to sell the treatments though?"

"Of course, that's precisely what I'm saying. Have you met Stitchum and the rest of the sales team down there?"

"Well, yes, of course, I spent the two weeks training down there with Stitchum; he was the one that explained how it all works."

"Right, well you obviously realise what I'm talking about. I've nothing personally against him, but if you keep calling a customer 'sir' after every sentence, or 'madam' as the case may be: I think they would quickly show you the door. Or in Stitchum's case: 'Good evening sir. Is this your house sir? I have reason to believe that you have woodworm attacking your property from a northerly direction', etc. If you were to start trying to employ the sales pressure and hard sell tactics that they use, people here would just laugh at your complete lack of subtlety."

"Yes, yes, I see what you mean."

Quite a reasonable observation I thought. However, given the fact that he'd been perceptive enough to recognise these obvious nuances; I couldn't help wondering why it was that the operative's were being paid and sent home through lack of work on what appeared to be a regular basis. Connum was no doubt just as keen to sell the companies' dubious treatments as the villains in Southampton. Had it occurred to Felix that Connum's alcohol problem might *just* have something to do with it? A further cause for concern as far as I could see was the fact that Felix seemed quite content sitting in his nice warm office drinking coffee and drawing up graphs, rather than getting out there and selling the treatments. I now realised what Tim Martin was talking about and quickly understood why his days were numbered. The position or more correctly, his position became even clearer when we looked at the 'work planning board'.

This was a much smaller version of the one in Southampton although the basic principal remained the same. It was ruled off into boxes with the days of the month along the top and the operative's names written down the side of it. Things weren't good. There had been very little work going on for the previous two weeks. Today showed two men working, one man working the next day, and nothing written on there for the rest of the month.

"You can see now why the boss's wanted another inspector up here," Felix remarked. "We're hoping that with another pair of hands we can turn this around. At the moment Connum is run off his feet trying to do the inspections that come in, and of course I'm stuck here in the office. Not that I want to be, but obviously I can't just leave Daphne here by herself."

"Oh well let's hope I can help," I said.

Felix and Connum were both sacked the following morning. I arrived at the office at eight o'clock and saw TM's black BMW parked on the pavement outside. Andrew was pacing up and down the office like a cheetah.

"You're late. What's the reason?" he said to me.

"No I'm not late," I said, "Felix told me to be here for eight. According to my watch it's exactly eight o'clock."

No one had spoken to me in this way since I was a teenager. The blood pumped around my head at an alarming rate. It took all of my self control not to react.

"Well Felix is no longer here, neither for that matter is Connum. Grab yourself a coffee and we'll run through with you exactly how we propose to reorganise this bloody pantomime."

Still feeling extremely angry by his previous remark, and finding his aggressive attitude intolerable, I couldn't help myself. I walked slowly over to where he was standing and said: "Look Andrew, before you go any further, you need to get one thing straight. Whatever has or has not transpired here is absolutely nothing whatsoever to do with me. If you want me to stay here and work for you I suggest you talk to me in a civilised manner."

Everything went deadly quiet for a few seconds. He face was purple: a vein in his neck had expanded and appeared to be visibly throbbing and pulsating with rage. He stared at me with total incomprehension.

"Yeah, point taken," he said. "Sorry Clive, I wasn't meaning to have a go at you. This farce up here has been getting at me for months. I'm just angry that we've allowed it to go on for so long."

"Okay, no hard feelings," I said, which was of course quite untrue.

"Alright ladies," TM said, "now you've sorted that out let's get down to business".

Daphne arrived looking like a frightened mouse; she seemed to sense that all was not well. Any planned tonsil inspections this morning would have to be put on hold. Andrew poked his head around the door of the erstwhile office of Felix and told her to make three coffees and bring them in.

"There's going to be a few changes here as from today. Don't worry 'luv', we'll let you know what's going on a bit later," he said to her in a failed attempt at trying to sound pleasant and relaxed.

At that moment the operatives (who they'd completely forgotten about) arrived.

"Right lads," Andrew said, "as you all know we've been having a few problems up here, no one has been pulling their weight and because of that we can't keep you anymore. You'll all be paid up until the end of the week but now you're free to go. Make sure you park the vans up properly outside. Don't remove anything from them that doesn't belong to you and bring the keys back up here to me. Do you all understand?"

After several perplexed primitive grunts, some throat clearing and snorting, they sauntered out of the office.

It was now down to business. TM was sitting at Felix's desk with Andrew and me sitting opposite desperately trying not to look at each other.

"We were going to wait until the end of the month, TM stated, to give you a chance to find your feet, but from our point of view it seemed quite ridiculous allowing this fiasco go on a day more than necessary. I'm sure you will have been able to see what we're talking about. Now: do you think you're up to running this branch if we put another inspector here to assist you?" he asked.

"Well, I'd be prepared to give it a go," I replied without really thinking. "Presumably there would be some sort of salary increment?"

"Yup," initially we'll pay you the same rate we were paying Felix. In addition to that you will receive five per cent of the target turnover. You can also take the car Felix had. It's a good car it's only three months old."

"How much is the target turnover here?" I asked.

"I'm surprised you haven't figured that out," Andrew interrupted. "It works on exactly the same principal as Southampton. You've got, or should I say, will have four operatives here. Each one is charged out at a minimum of two hundred pounds a day: that's exactly four grand a week."

"Okay, but what happens if it's not possible to reach that figure? I presume I follow Felix down the road?"

"No. No. No." TM interjected, sensing my cynicism. "That won't happen. It's both in your interests and ours that you make a go of it. If you try, and give it your best shot we'll give you all the support and encouragement you need."

"Right, Okay. Thank you. I'll see what I can do."

It was decided to allow two weeks for this proposed magical turn around to take effect. No further work would be booked in during this 'restructuring' period. All future treatments would commence two weeks hence. According to Andrew this would allow me enough time to fill the board with work for the following month, and interview and employ four new 'decent' operatives. Their plan was that Stitchum would be sent up to assist me until they could train another inspector. Stitchum and I would for the next two weeks 'go hell for leather' to get work in from every inspection that we carried out. An operative would be sent up from Southampton to carry out the job that was booked in tomorrow, and as far as they saw it the whole plan would run like clockwork.

Needless to say, I didn't exactly share their optimism or enthusiasm. I wanted them both to go. I wanted to go as well. I'd now had enough of their overbearing and intimidating presence.

Daphne now looked like a grey pinched nervous rabbit, neurotically shuffling papers around, and continually moving her keyboard from one position to another. She was instructed to give me the inspection sheets for the day, and was ineffectively reassured that 'her' job with the company was quite safe. Vacuous as she was; she didn't believe them, and neither did I. Thankfully they decided that enough of their valuable time had been spent on this particular axing operation, and they left.

I was half an hour late for the first inspection; not that it mattered, the person who'd requested it had forgotten all about it. The others; six in total, were all relatively straightforward. I'd managed to book three of them in, two of which were floor replacements, and the third was a new damp course and replastering. I'd already decided that I wouldn't under any circumstances employ the sort of under hand tactics I had witnessed in Southampton. If the people wanted the work doing that was fine. If they didn't that was also fine as far as I was concerned. This approach seemed to work. It was of course helpful knowing the area and generally feeling more relaxed away from the hungry den of thieves in Southampton. My initial euphoria at getting the work in so easily was tempered with the thought that I had yet to interview and employ the men to do it. This in itself wouldn't have been too much of a problem. The problem was that Sprayum and Scarper would only pay a pittance for unskilled people that had no idea of what they were doing. All the problems that were undoubtedly going to arise from this simple fact were going to be mine, and mine alone.

By five o'clock I had drafted the various reports out which were now waiting in the lovely Daphne's tray to be typed up. A quick look through the diary at the next day's inspections revealed that only four were booked in. Under the circumstances, I couldn't quite see why it would be necessary for me to have Stitchum's dedicated assistance with these. I phoned the head office number and asked the singing Jill at the other end if I could speak to TM. "Just a moment," the voice sang out "I'll put you through."

"Hello, what's the problem?" he asked.

"There's no problem," I replied. "Tomorrow there are only four inspections. I can do these. There is no need for you to send Stitchum up here."

"Right," he said, "how did you get on today?"

"Fine, no problem," I said. "Got three definite jobs in; two are complete floor replacements, and the third one is a new damp course and replastering."

"That's good work 'lad', keep it up, and phone me again about the same time tomorrow."

Chapter Eight

The next day brought a similar degree of success. TM seemed quite delighted with the progress being made. He told me that an advert had been placed in my local paper for operatives. The advert suggested they should phone me for an interview. It was whilst carrying out these interviews that my doubts and fears were confirmed. The people I saw; a rag tag lot of unskilled people drifting from one dead end job to another, most of whom had absolutely no building experience, didn't actually fill me with confidence. Laughably one of them had to be capable of plastering. Of all the men I interviewed, twenty four in total, only two thought they might be able to construct a new floor; but both of them admitted to never having attempted anything like it before. None of them had ever attempted plastering. One of them a Scottish fellow called Craig gave a wry smile and told me in no uncertain terms that if he could plaster walls, he'd be living a good life somewhere with a bad woman and never ending crates of whiskey. Up until this point, although being very sceptical about the whole operation; I did still have a glimmer of hope that the hierarchy would see the light and pay the going rate for some proper skilled trades and avoid a multitude of problems that were inevitably bound to occur.

This glimmer was quickly extinguished. I knew a number of skilled and competent people: carpenters, plasterers, bricklayers etc, who they could have used, and at this particular time they would have been pleased with the work; but they simply wouldn't be persuaded to pay them.

I had now been enjoying the delights of my new position eight whole days. I was quite sorry that they had decided to retain Daphne's services as she was now seriously getting on my nerves. As the interviews were being conducted I was forced to listen to her opinion as to why a particular person 'looked alright' to her, and why so and so seemed a nice bloke etc, etc. Either by luck or judgement or whatever, I had managed to book the first three weeks of the next month which was December which meant I had achieved exactly what they wanted and without assistance from the intrepid Stitchum.

A further advert was placed in the local paper, and Andrew, having reached the conclusion that I was incapable of employing anyone; came up for three days to interview the various candidates. According to him he had found no difficulty whatsoever in finding four 'good practical men'. Realising now that things were drawing to a close I phoned TM and advised him that I didn't intend to hang around to try and sort the problems out that were inevitably bound to happen. Despite all his attempts to try and convince me that I'd somehow got it wrong, I couldn't be persuaded. I could see the nightmare unfolding, and was effectively quite impotent to do anything to prevent it. I gave the office keys, and the car keys to Daphne as instructed and walked out. A massive weight, a feeling of impending doom had suddenly been lifted. I was light headed and euphoric; no more Sprayum and Scarper. No more TM, Andrew or Daphne. I felt as if I had been brainwashed, and was now regaining my senses and self worth as I walked home in the rain with a definite spring in my step.

That evening, still feeling slightly euphoric at my new found freedom I decided to relax with a decent bottle of wine and some Mozart playing gently in the background. My peace however was soon interrupted with the shrill ringing of the telephone. I'd decided not to answer it wanting to savour my alcohol induced tranquillity but the bloody thing wouldn't stop. In the end after God knows how many rings, I got up and picked it up.

"Clive, its Tim."

"Oh hell," I thought. "Hello, good evening," I said having been taken by complete surprise.

"Can you come down to the office here tomorrow morning? I think we need to have a chat."

"Well...I don't know, to be quite honest... I don't think there's anything we can chat about. You've made your position clear, and I'm simply not prepared to be the fall guy for all the problems you are storing up for yourselves."

"Yes, yes, I understand how you feel and I think we can come up with a solution that will work for both of us. Look, I can't stay on the phone now, come down at about ten tomorrow and we'll run through it all then."

"Okay," I said, "see you then. Goodnight."

Shit. Shit. Shit. What have I just agreed to I thought. Within seconds I was back underneath a black cloud again. Why the hell did I agree to this? It's completely pointless. This could have been sorted out a few moments ago. Having experienced a few hours of freedom, I really didn't want to get entwined with this insidious duo again. Yes, but be sensible I told myself. At least go and see the man and listen to what he's got to say. After all it's an olive branch; perhaps whatever he's got in mind could work. Until you actually go and talk to him face to face you'll never know. You've at least got to do this. That, I knew was the positive argument. On the negative side, I knew that I had stepped out of line. I was a rebel, a maverick; I'd dared to question and answer back, stand up for myself. This to them was completely unacceptable. In the long term they wouldn't tolerate this sort of flagrant disrespect. My days would be numbered. My head was now spinning. I finished off the last of the wine and tried unsuccessfully to get some sleep.

The murderous two and a half hour crawl down to Southampton in the rush hour traffic the following morning allowed me a little more time to think. Trying to keep an open mind was virtually impossible. The 'beginners' luck I'd had in getting the work in and meeting their sales target had no doubt impressed them. They weren't going to let me go that easily. The failing branch office at Brighton had in their eyes been suddenly and miraculously brought back to life. I knew that they would within reason, at least for the moment, do whatever they could to placate my arrogant whims. But in the long term they would be delighted to see the back of me for daring to question the methods that for them had proved to be so lucrative. Well, I'm nearly there now I thought, let's get this over with.

The singing Jill showed me into TM's office and swished out leaving a pungent aroma of cheap perfume. He was on the telephone and signalled to me to sit down. The conversation he was having was something to do with his golf membership. Finally this ended. He put the phone down; got up and proffered the bunch of bananas which this time were a strange crimson colour.

"Thanks for coming in," he said. "Coffee?"

"Erm...yeah, that would be good."

"Now, I understand your concerns; the problem we've got is that if we were to pay the sort of prohibitive rates that a lot of these tradesmen you're talking about want; we simply wouldn't make any money. None of the operatives we employ here has a trade as such. If they did they wouldn't be working here; they'd be literally earning three times as much somewhere else. Are you with me?" He asked, looking at me as if I hadn't been able to grasp this.

"Yes, of course . . . I understand what you're saying but with respect you're wrong."

His face contorted into a pained grimace. His reply was put on hold whilst Jill placed a tray of fresh roasted coffee on the desk with a plate of artistically arranged biscuits.

"Why am I wrong?" He asked.

"Okay, I'll tell you why you're wrong." I didn't actually care now. I had nothing to lose, apart from the job; which I didn't want now anyway. "Take an example of a floor replacement: you put two unskilled monkeys on it in the hope that they will do a professional job for a third of the price you would have to pay skilled people. In practice what happens is that they take three times as long to do it and completely mess it up. You haven't made any sort of saving doing it this way. The chances are that even after it's finished, further works will be required to sort out a multitude of problems that are bound to occur. By which time the client's patience and your credibility will have completely dissipated. The whole point is that I am not prepared to take the flack for all the cock ups that are inevitably going to happen."

His face had become larger somehow and had taken on a light crimson hue. He lit a cigarette and exhaled a tunnel of blue smoke which settled just above my head. He was clearly rattled but was looking for some sort of compromise.

"Hmm, well, how would you feel if we allowed you to use a limited number of skilled people for these sort of jobs? The operatives that Andrew has taken on could assist with the unskilled parts. You know; the clearing out of the old floor, the labouring, the fetching and carting of materials etc, we don't need to pay skilled people to do this do we?"

"No, that sounds workable. They could also be used to hack off plaster, and once you have given them some kind of training down here, they could then carry out woodworm treatments and install chemical damp courses and so on."

"Have you got any people in mind then?" He asked.

"Well, some of the trades that used to work for me are probably still looking for work. I can ask them."

"Friends of yours are they?"

"No, they're not friends of mine. There's nothing devious going on. I know a few carpenters and plasterers that produce good work, and their rates certainly aren't exorbitant."

"Right then, that's what we'll do. Can we leave it to you to organise this?"

"Yeah, I will. There is one question though, how to we go about paying these men?"

"Who do you mean 'your' people?" he said.

"Yes."

"They need to send an invoice into us here. It needs to detail the job they have been working on, the hours spent there, and their hourly rate. Once we've got that it'll go through the system, and they'll get paid at the end of the following month."

"Ah, that might be a problem."

"Why?" he asked aggressively.

"Well, if we were to use the people I know; that would mean them working for the first week or two of December, and not getting paid until the end of January. If you consider that most of these people have been unemployed for a while; the prospect of them having to wait until the end of January with Christmas in the middle . . . if you see what I mean."

This was just about the last straw. He was clearly now at the end of his tether.

"Okay once they've done what they have to do; send their invoices down here; mark them for my attention, and I'll send you their cheques back by return."

"Right okay . . . thanks." I said, as if he were doing me a great personal favour.

"I'm leaving it to you though to make sure that you limit the amount of time they spend on site. I don't want them doing any work that our own men could be doing."

"No, I understand."

"Well, do you feel happier about the situation now?" he asked.

"Yes, it's good to get things sorted out."

"Right, if you get anymore problems give me a ring. I'm always here at the end of the phone. Now that we've got this sorted out; keep the work coming in 'lad'."

I shook hands again with the crimson bananas, and left feeling tense and angry at what had just transpired. I felt like a spoilt child that had dug its heels in and thrown a series of tantrums to get its own way. Although I had got my point across, it was clear he didn't agree with what I was saying, but in the end had no choice but to acquiesce to my demands. He no doubt thought he was doing me a favour. Having a nasty suspicious mind, he undoubtedly thought I would be getting some sort of kick back from the 'friends' that I gave the work to.

Daphne fired one question after another. Evidently Stitchum had come up to do the inspections that were booked and would be returning shortly. Oh God, I thought not more questions. I really didn't want to be here now. I should have left things the way they were, my first decision was the right decision. I needed to phone around the carpenters and plasterers I knew, to see if they were available for the following week. The nagging awareness that I should be delighted that they had allowed me to do this prevented me from picking up the phone. I was now feeling a sort pernicious and hopeless despair. Out of perversity I wanted to introduce the 'buggerment' factor into the proceedings. If I now went along with the new plan; even if things ran smoothly, they would be grumbling and complaining that all their profit on the jobs had been lost to 'my men'. Part of me wanted to phone TM and say that I couldn't get hold of anyone; that they were all busy, and allow the cowboys that Andrew had employed to do their worst and cause utter mayhem. Eventually after having satiated Daphne's curiosity I forced myself to do it and quickly found enough people to start the following Monday.

When Stitchum returned I had to endure the equivalent of a forty minute police interview. He seemed to regard me now with a great deal of suspicion; unable to believe that I had stood up for myself. According to him all the inspections he'd carried out were a total waste of time. The people in Sussex were all 'snobs', all 'with their noses in the air'. When he tried to talk to them, they apparently turned away and told him to send his report in, and they'd let him know their decision in due course.

"Quite a successful day then?" I suggested.

"Not exactly, I'm pleased you've got things sorted out though. I don't particularly want to come up here again," he confessed. "Mind you mate, your cards are marked. When Andrew finds out what's happened, he'll think about nothing else except getting rid of you as quickly as he can, I know that for a fact."

"Yes I know that's precisely how I see it, but who knows, I might just last until Christmas."

"I wouldn't put money on it." he said with his knowing coppers stare, and made a hasty retreat.

Having organised the labour for the next three weeks, things progressed on a fairly straight forward basis. I continued to carry out inspections, supervise the work in progress and tried not to dwell too much on what had so far transpired. My run of good fortune continued and I managed to book the whole of January. Andrew complained continuously about the sums being paid out to 'my men' without ever having compared the costs of using 'his men'. Trying to explain that there was absolutely no difference in cost; and that the work was being completed more quickly and efficiently using skilled labour was completely lost on him. Just before Christmas he'd hurriedly cobbled together a new price structure for my benefit which increased the labour rates I should charge for floor replacements and plastering by fifty per cent to cover the cost of using 'my men'. Extraordinarily, this made little or no difference to securing the jobs, although it did of course mean that they were making much greater profits than before.

Thankfully the whole dubious enterprise shut down for two weeks over the Christmas period which was a welcome respite. I was never paid the 'target bonus' they'd promised despite exceeding this by twenty per cent. According to Andrew the Brighton branch had lost money having to pay so much out to 'my men'. A further operative was employed by Andrew to add to the four who were already hanging around the office every morning. I quickly realised that this was quite a cunning move on his part which meant that having five men to find work for, meant my target had increased from four to five thousand pounds a week. This new figure would have been virtually unachievable unless I worked twelve hour days, seven days a week. I knew that if I did somehow manage this; a sixth one would appear and so on.

The fact remained that this was still quite a lucrative business. During the fifteen years I had run my own small building company I had managed to make a reasonable living but nothing more. I didn't seem to have any problem getting the work in, but the profits were nothing compared to the mark up that Sprayum and Scarper were trousering. After mulling over this for several weeks I decided I would start my own timber preservation business. The only *slight* problem was the capital required. As the pressure increased from Andrew and TM for me to achieve ever increasing sales targets, I became more obsessed with this idea. This had to be my way out and the logical way forward.

Most of my evenings were spent trying to work out how much I needed. I calculated the cost of a months rent on a small office, the deposit on a van, a months salary for a receptionist, the same for an operative, printing, stationary, plant, equipment, advertising; the list seemed endless. In the end I arrived at an absurdly optimistic figure of ten thousand pounds. This would get the thing up and running with all costs covered for the first month. If I managed to have the same luck getting the work in as I'd had with Sprayum and Scarper, there would be no looking back. Having decided to do this now; every day of going to the office became more and more intolerable. The problem of course was where could I get the money from?

After putting a few 'feelers' out to old clients I used to do work for; and receiving the same negative response I was becoming quite despondent. Most of the developers I knew had either been forced out of business by their friendly bank managers, or were struggling to survive under the current economic conditions. I then remembered an elderly fellow called Harry Wiseman. I'd last spoken to him about ten years ago. Harry was a fly character with a finger in many pies. For a number of years I used to carry out the conversion and maintenance work on a number of houses he owned. He also owned a chain of betting shops, greengrocery shops and God knows what else. Despite being a wily old sod, I'd always had a good working relationship with him. The contracts I had carried out for him were always completed on time and I'd always stuck rigidly to whatever price I had quoted. He had to be worth a try.

That evening I ran through the figures again trying to see if I had forgotten anything. I didn't really need to do this, I'd run through it so many times before. Harry was my last hope. I picked up the phone and put it down again. No, I can't do this I thought, this is ridiculous; clutching at straws. Go on, do it, I said to myself, after all he can only say no. I walked up and down the room a few more times, drank another glass of wine, and then picked up the phone again; dialled his number and waited. After about ten rings his wife answered.

"Hello, this is the Wiseman residence," she said in a croaky voice.

"Oh good evening, I wonder if it's possible to speak to Harry. This is Clive West."

"Clive who?"

"Clive West."

"Does he know you?" she enquired.

"Yes he does."

"What's it in connection with?" she asked suspiciously.

"Erm... well it's a personal matter . . . I used to do some work for your husband."

117

"Wait. I'll get him for you."

"Allo Clive," Harry shouted down the phone in his sixty a day bronchial voice; talk about a blast from the past. How are you?"

"I'm fine, how are you keeping?"

"Oh much the same really, I'm still hiding from the tax man, trying to keep body and soul together. Mind you, nice as it is to hear from you I'm sure you haven't phoned to enquire about my health, what's up?"

I explained to him about my bank manager's indecent exposure, and that I was now working for Sprayum and Scarper, and my idea of starting my own woodworm company.

"Sounds like a bloody good idea to me," he said. "You'll never make any money working for anyone else as you well know."

"No that's right," I agreed. "My only problem is trying to raise the cash to get it off the ground."

"Ah so that's why you've phoned me. How much do you need?" he asked.

"Well, I reckon I can do it on ten grand."

"Hmm...Ten grand," he said, "that's not very much."

"I know," I said, now seriously doubting my own calculations.

"What happens if it all goes tits up?" he asked. "You're not going to be able to pay me back are you?"

"No, I guess not."

"Well, I tell you what I'd be prepared to do. I'll give you the ten grand for a twenty five per cent share of the new company. If it goes to the wall, I'll just write it off as bad judgement. If the whole thing takes off then I'll have backed a winner, and we both come out of it smelling of roses. How does that sound to you?"

"That sounds good to me." I said trying to contain myself. "What about interest on it. The ten grand I mean?"

"No, it's interest free. I won't charge you interest. You either make it or you don't. I hope you do of course for both our sakes."

"Well, what can I say? Thanks a lot Harry; I'll get the wheels in motion."

"That's all right mate, I've no doubt the wife will tell me that I need my bumps feeling but everyone's got to start somewhere. Come round and see me when you've got the forms for the new company: we'll fill them in, issue the share certificates and all the rest of it and I'll give you a cheque. You'll need to think of a name of course and open a bank account for it before I can do that. The cheque I give you will need to be payable to the new company for tax reasons. I can offset a bit of what the vultures are trying to claw from me at the moment."

"Yeah, I understand, I'll ring you again in a few days when the forms come through, and thanks again Harry."

"YES...YES...YES. Cracked it." I shouted to myself. A name, yes a name, I'd already thought about this. It was going to be called 'The Ethical Preservation Company'. Mine would be the only honourable woodworm company in existence. A company people would trust, where there were no slick salesmen masquerading as inspectors and 'surveyors' lying through their teeth to sell unnecessary and expensive treatments. I might even persuade the pope to bless its inauguration. I'd show them that honesty and fairness will succeed in the end.

It was now the beginning of January. I knew there was no point handing my notice in as Sprayum and Scarper never allowed anyone to work through a notice period. They were paranoid. Anyone deciding to leave their employ must be ejected immediately. They feared probably quite justifiably, that the disgruntled employee might take their revenge for all the injustices inflicted upon them and carry out some malicious act whilst they still had the chance. Needing every penny I could find and not wishing to break into Harry's money too soon: I decided to get all the preparations under way with a view to starting 'The Ethical Preservation Company' on the first day of February. Knowing my days there really were numbered, nothing now that was said or done by Andrew or TM had any effect on me whatsoever. It was very much like having an invisible suit of armour. I registered the new company and opened a bank account at Harry's bank; his introduction being invaluable allowing me to skirt around the usual in depth inquisition.

The office I found consisted of one and a half rooms at the rear of a launderette: the walls of which were running with dampness and had an outside toilet in a yard at the side. These prestigious premises were the cheapest I could find. It was at least a high street address and rent free for the first quarter on condition that I cured the damp problem. I contract hired a new van and had it sign written. Things were now really starting to knit together. All the printing and stationary was ordered, the office furnished with cheap second hand furniture and the two grubby telephones there were cleaned and reconnected. Two more weeks to go before 'D' day, it just remained to find a receptionist and organise some limited marketing and advertising.

It was around this time that Daphne was mysteriously stricken with 'tummy problems'. I received a phone call from her early one morning when she described in detail, a plethora of strange and unnerving symptoms, which according to her heralded the onset of some highly infectious and probably fatal diseases. Judging from her alarming symptoms it seemed unlikely that any form of recovery was possible for at least a few years which meant some sort of contingency measures needed to be activated.

I was instructed by TM to phone around the secretarial agencies and negotiate a rate for a 'temp' to cover for Daphne. There really wasn't much negotiating to do: most of the agencies needed at least a week's notice, and their rates certainly weren't open to negotiation. The last one I tried however came up with Gloria.

When she arrived, I thought for a moment that I'd mistakenly phoned an escort agency rather than a secretarial agency. She certainly couldn't be accused of over dressing. I had I suppose become accustomed to the shapeless Daphne, clad in her sombre rather conservative attire. Gloria's skimpy garments and her adequate contours came as quite a shock early in the morning. I spent the next hour with her explaining what we did, how to book appointments with clients and how to prepare reports. Every phone call that came in after that resulted in her clumping across to my office in her five inch stilettos, poking her appendages around the door, and explaining the problems the clients had. This seemed to cover a fairly wide spectrum from 'this geezer on the phone's got something nasty fungus growing in his back passage' and do we treat that? To 'this ole' gal' on the phone's got maggots or 'summink' in her drawers', can we go round there and have a look at them?

At least Gloria was a lot more pleasant to look at than the dreary Daphne, and added some much needed colour to the depressing surroundings. She also had an excellent sense of humour and picked up things fairly quickly. For a woman in her late twenties, she'd had an interesting life: having been a dancer, a croupier, a singer in an all female rock band, and latterly a magician's assistant for a stage act that had travelled around the country. This promising career came to an abrupt end when 'The Amazing Marvello' she accompanied died on stage from cirrhosis. After the third day Daphne phoned and confirmed that despite her gloomy predictions, she had made a miraculous recovery and would return to work the next day. As Gloria and I seemed to get on together, and this was going to be my last chance, I asked her if she would consider leaving the agency and work for The Ethical Preservation Company. I explained that I could guarantee a months work, but things very much depended on work coming in for the new company to survive. Having a light hearted philosophical outlook, and possibly being unwisely impetuous, she agreed instantly and seemed quite excited and enthusiastic about the whole venture.

As my time with Sprayum and Scarper drew to a close, I signed up with one of the chemical companies as an 'Approved Contractor' and ordered some equipment and a small supply of chemical. As part of this deal, they supplied a pad of impressive looking thirty year guarantee certificates which I would issue to my clients. A number of adverts were placed in local newspapers announcing the birth of The Ethical Preservation Company. Harry's money just seemed to evaporate. All that was now left was enough to pay Gloria for the first month, and enough to pay an operative for the first few weeks. I was relying on my last month's salary from Sprayum and Scarper to cover any other unforeseen costs that might arise including my own living expenses. Harry's comment that ten grand wasn't very much kept springing to mind, but now there was no turning back.

With just a short time left, the days seemed endless. I kept rehearsing my parting speech and dreaded having to make that final telephone call. How would I actually word it? I couldn't explain that I was starting my own woodworm company, not only would this incite them to murder: they would quite definitely withhold the salary due to me which I needed now more than ever. I decided to explain that I'd decided to start another small building company, at least this had an element of truth about it, and they of course were bound to come across The Ethical Preservation Company's advertising which hopefully would be after my final salary cheque had cleared.

I should have realised that nothing ever goes according to plan. On the last day at lunch time, I received a phone call from Andrew explaining that he was on his way over to me with a new sales consultant they had hired: some slick smooth talking American swine called 'Vance', and that Vance was

122

going to spend the next few weeks with me in Brighton. He would evidently help me to achieve my new sales target by accompanying me on the inspections I had and would then after each inspection; carry out a forensic analysis of my technique, or lack of it as Andrew seemed to infer. Out of masochistic perversity I desperately wanted to meet Vance. The description conjured up just about everything I had always instinctively detested about these sorts of people, but I now had to seize the moment and burst Andrew's balloon.

"That's very kind of you," I said, "but I have decided I want to leave."

"Leave?" what are you talking about?" he said.

"Working for other people isn't for me I'm afraid, I've had enough."

"What's happened?" he asked incredulously.

"Nothing in particular, its simply not for me. I guess I've spent too long working for myself and running my own business. I now can't adjust to being told what to do."

"Look, stay where you are," he said with an obvious note of panic in his voice, "we'll be right over."

The office door was open during this conversation with Daphne obviously having listened in. When I walked back out to make some coffee she stared at me timidly as if I had suddenly morphed into some kind of psychotic maniac.

After what seemed like a lifetime, Andrew and Vance appeared. Vance was exactly how I'd imagined him; overdressed, over fed, and oozing with confidence; a small obnoxious sort of character with an enormous ego and very little else. Andrew was clearly angry that I had turned out to be an unstable arrogant lunatic that was about to walk away from a promising career.

The now terrified Daphne was instructed to make coffee for us as we retreated into my tiny office.

"Right, there's got to be more to it," Andrew said looking at me with hatred in his eyes."

"It's as I told you," I said, "it's really no more complicated than that."

"Well, you've cost us a considerable amount of money, and now you somehow think it's perfectly alright just to walk away. We've treated you fairly, you're not exactly treating us with the same degree of fairness and respect are you?"

I could see he was rearing for a fight or at least an extremely heated argument, both of which would be utterly futile. I just wanted to go as quickly as possible and refused to be goaded.

"I'm sorry if you think that I've behaved improperly," I said, "but I've made my decision. I want to leave and that's it I'm afraid."

His face had turned a strange puce colour; his right eyelid was twitching in synchronisation with the corner of his lip. He seemed to be totally lost for words. After a pause of a few seconds which seemed to me like several minutes he said very quietly, "Give me your car keys, and the office keys."

I placed them both on the desk in front of him and waited cautiously to see what was going to happen next. The tension in the air was extremely powerful, not that dissimilar to sitting on top of an unexploded bomb

He very slowly put the keys into his pocket, raised himself off the chair and instructed me with all the dignity and self control he could muster to 'fuck off '.

Chapter Nine

I think drunk with euphoria would be an apt description of how I felt having finally escaped the clutches of Sprayum and Scarper. Whatever happened now, I would never be subjected to that loathsome form of intimidation and humiliation that every poor employee of theirs had to endure on a daily basis. The Ethical Preservation Company might possibly go under after a short time but I knew now that I would rather die of starvation than ever contemplate another similar move. The very idea of 'sales targets' and the various iniquitous forms of threats and pressure that were an inherent constituent of this loathsome phrase was totally abhorrent. I would now set out to prove that these destructors of the remnants of human morality were unnecessary and were purely the manifestation of mans insatiable greed. I had of course to somehow equate these finer sensibilities with some sort of business plan or I would surely go to the dogs.

It was now two o'clock on a wet, grey and blustery Friday afternoon. I walked along the windswept main road in the direction of my new office which was no more than a hundred yards away: bought some fish and chips and half a bottle of champagne from the off licence on the corner and retreated to the safety of this new sanctuary.

Sitting there on my rickety second hand 'directors chair' (a 'bargain' at ten pounds) in the freezing cold and gloom after my lone celebration: the pervading stench of dampness and chip fat invading my senses; I began to panic at the

125

thought of Gloria arriving at nine o'clock on Monday morning expecting to work in a vibrant busy environment, when in reality, no one at this point knew of our existence. I was beginning to question my whole motivation behind this blindly ambitious venture which I knew in all honesty was born out of a ridiculous moral outrage that I seemed to becoming obsessed with.

Pointless worrying about that at this stage, I thought, I must be positive and use the available time productively. After all there were a series of expensive adverts appearing in the local newspapers the following week announcing the arrival of The Ethical Preservation Company with a twenty five per cent discount on all new estimates until the end of the month. I also now had boxes of brochures sitting in the office that had been printed extolling the virtues of 'the only honest woodworm company on the south coast'. These, I had planned would be distributed in little plastic stands to estate agents, surveyors, solicitors, and anyone remotely connected with the sale of properties. The best thing to do now would be to start delivering them, and at the same time hopefully pick up requests for inspections from some of the estate agents.

I picked up the new sign written van which I thought would add a little credence to my mission, placed the brochures and the stands in the back and set about this task. Apart from a few odious gelled haired specimens in tight fitting Armani suits, the agents I visited all seemed reasonably pleasant and receptive and were certainly interested in the discount that was being offered. The ethical side of my new company didn't seem to be of much interest to them. I should have perhaps realised that not many of them understood what 'ethical' meant anyway. Amazingly I managed to pick up five inspections during this process. After nearly four hours I had managed to cover over sixty estate agents and had virtually lost my voice after trying to explain to each one why my new company was unique, and the reasons why they should consider recommending its services. I certainly didn't enjoy this exercise, I'd always detested this insidious type of sales patter, but I knew it was an essential part of getting the business off the ground.   Buzzing with adrenalin, I returned to the office to phone the five people the agents came up with in the hope of getting the first job in. This was far more problematical than I had imagined. The first one I phoned was suspicious and quite aggressive.

"Ethical what?" he said.

"The Ethical Preservation Company."

"Never heard of it," he replied.

"It's Clive West from The Ethical Preservation Company, we specialise in damp proofing and woodworm treatments."

"Never heard of you! Who gave you my phone number? What do you want?"

"Floggum and Smarmy, the estate agents gave me your number, they said you were looking for quotes to do some damp proofing at the house you were buying from them."

"What's your name again?"

"The Ethical Preservation Company."

"How long have you been around then?"

"We've just started," I replied.

"Well... I don't know, are you one of these 'here today and gone tomorrow' set ups? To be quite honest I don't know who to trust anymore. I think you're all a lot of bloody villains."

"I'm sorry you feel like that sir," I said, "Ours is the only ethical preservation company around. We only quote for work that is absolutely necessary: you may well find that our quote is cheaper than the others you've had, but of course it's entirely up to you."

Eventually I managed to arrange an appointment with him the following morning. This first enquiry wasn't a particularly good omen for the future but at least it got the thing started, and represented quite a challenge for what possibly lay ahead.

The next lead from Greaseball and Weasel was much easier. They'd already spoken to their client explaining that I would be calling them, and so the next appointment was booked an hour later. After what seemed like hours of explaining and justifying my position, I succeeded in booking the other three, all at one hourly intervals the next morning. I thought that whether or not any of these visits actually resulted in 'jobs' was not really too important at this stage. Doing the five inspections on Saturday and drafting out the reports and estimates for Gloria to type up on Monday was a sound psychological advancement and somehow injected an element of realism into the dream. At least for the first day of trading there would be the feeling that we were busy: something was happening: Gloria would be tapping away on the old second hand word processor I had bought, and with any luck the telephones would start ringing with enquiries generated from the newspaper adverts. The prospect of securing even two of the jobs and having some work in progress was now becoming a reality.

On Sunday evening it occurred to me that I ought to have at least one or two people lined up to actually carry out the treatments. I phoned around speaking to various people that had worked for me and who had stepped in to assist Sprayum and Scarper. One of the carpenters I knew Keith, had a brother called Ben who had previously worked for Killemall, the large woodworm and damp proofing company that had employed Felix; and Ben was evidently was looking for a job. This could be very useful, assuming things went according to plan. It was agreed that he would contact me to discuss this amazing 'career opportunity'.

Within what seemed just a blink of the eye Monday morning arrived. A scantily clad Gloria was perched on her 'new' five pound chair, the broken back of which was secured with duct tape, bashing the reports out and answering a surprising spate of phone calls in her cheery estuarine voice. For some strange reason better known to her, the company was now called 'effycool preservations'. Perhaps she thought this was less stodgy and formal than my title. She was certainly very friendly and willing to listen sympathetically to a wide range of strange problems that people had or thought they'd discovered with their properties. Her stock phrase appeared to be 'Oh don't worry, we'll sort the problem out for you and you'll get a 'sirstiffykit' for thirty years once we done the work for you'. The quality that was most endearing about her was her enthusiasm and unsuppressed optimism that the company would succeed: something I found difficult to share with her at this juncture knowing that on this first day of trading The Ethical Preservation Company was technically insolvent.

There was also the recurring worry that although Gloria's wages for the first four weeks were in the bank, together with two weeks wages for an operative, that was it: I had assets of precisely two pounds and forty nine pence to live on until my termination pay arrived from Sprayum and Scarper. I was hoping their cheque would be released to me before they spotted the adverts which were appearing as from today. Starting up as a competitor only a hundred yards or so from them: and particularly undercutting their prices by twenty five per cent, wasn't I realised, exactly something that was likely to engender their spirit of camaraderie. For the past week or so I hadn't slept properly. I'd been experiencing the most vivid dreams of a slow painful death from malnutrition and then Andrew, in a mad frenzy lobbing a grenade through the door of our new office resulting in a massive explosion with various parts of Gloria and myself being stuck to the ceiling, or of us both being kidnapped at gunpoint, tortured, and being forced to abandon this foolish venture.

By mid morning the five reports were completed and in a desperate attempt to secure my first job I decided to deliver them by hand. All of the clients were out except the last one. This was a quote for replacing rotten timber floors, damp proofing and re-plastering. Much to my amazement I was invited inside whilst the owner, a ruddy faced middle aged fellow, carefully undid the envelope and started scrutinizing the estimate.

"Hmm," he muttered, casting a furtive sidelong glance at me under his glasses and then picked up a cardboard file from the dining room table, opened it up and seemed to be comparing mine against the other estimates in the file.

"Hmm," he muttered again, "when could you start?"

"When would you like us to start?" I replied.

"Well, we'd really like to get this over and out of the way as quickly as possible so whenever you like."

"It should be possible tomorrow or the next day, I'm going back to the office now I'll check with our contracts manager, and perhaps I could phone you this evening to confirm?"

"Yup," that's fine, and thank you very much for being so prompt," he said.

"No problem," I said, "there is just one thing though, we do need you to sign the acceptance form which is attached to our estimate, and we also need a twenty five per cent deposit before I can book the work in."

"That's fine," he said, producing a cheque book and scribbled out a cheque for fifteen hundred pounds.

We shook hands, with me positively salivating at the renewed hope this injection of funds offered, and at the same time hoping he couldn't detect the sense of euphoria I felt at having secured the first deal. This was certainly living dangerously, but now: breathing space, that's what this meant. So it seems there is a God after all. The next challenge would be to open some trading accounts with timber yards and builders merchants which would allow me to 'book' all the materials and keep the fifteen hundred pounds, or most of it, to keep the business going until further jobs were in and completed. This was going to be difficult, but it had to be done. I already had accounts with most of the builder's merchants in the name of my previous building company. None of these would be ecstatic about granting me further credit whilst the old company still owed them thousands. Had Grimshaw my friendly bank manager allowed me to finish the various building contracts that were in progress, all of these people would have been paid, and the small business I had would have made a reasonable profit and gone on to do other jobs. I still found this injustice extremely difficult to come to terms with and just hoped that his indecent exposure had now been permanently curtailed.

Eventually I found two firms I'd never used before and applied for accounts with both of them. One of them agreed to 'fast track' the application which meant that all being well, the account would be open in three days time. Things were now looking more positive. Gloria was overjoyed at my apparent good fortune and even more delighted that during my absence; a total of seven inspections were booked for the next day, with four more the day after.

The inspection enquiry sheets I'd had printed required certain basic information to be entered into the respective boxes, which were the clients name, address, telephone number etc, with a separate section entitled 'type of inspection required'. In this area the type of problem needed to be described i.e.; woodworm, damp, dry rot, rotten floorboards, etc, etc. Gloria's comments and remarks did not somehow adhere strictly to this format. The inspection sheets in my tray had a strange variety of problems that seemed to exist from 'nasty things crawling everywhere', to something 'funny' growing out of the ceiling, and 'the whole place is alive with fleas or summink'. She obviously sensed the degree of urgency in getting some work in, no doubt imagining that whatever the person's problem was: 'effycool preservations' would come up with the answer.

The following morning Keith the carpenter I knew and his brother Ben arrived at the office to pick up the van and the details of the floor replacement job. Ben was delighted at the prospect of being employed as an operative despite my having made clear to him that the work we had was quite 'thin on the ground' (a euphemism of the finest order), and the position was not exactly pensionable at this stage.

Ben was a friendly emaciated fellow of twenty five that looked more like a starving poet than an operative, but evidently he had spent four years working for Killemall and seemed to know what he was talking about.

Trying to explain the details of the job they were about to do was a little difficult primarily because they're eyes were both firmly focused on Gloria's ample appendages. Eventually they reassured me that they knew where to go and what had to be done, made a further in depth study of what was being displayed by her and left.

Over the next few days the inspections came in at a steady pace with me adhering strictly to the ethical format of only quoting for work that was absolutely necessary. This was satisfying from a moral sense but was decidedly not profitable. It also created a whole plethora of complications, and in reality didn't seem to inspire confidence in the clients, many of whom had already received quotes from Sprayum and Scarper and many others. By trying to explain to them that for example; the treatments the other companies were proposing to carry out to certain areas of their property were not really necessary in most cases because the woodworm flight holes were old with no signs of any current activity: had the effect of confusing them, and casting doubt over my credibility. 'Well the other companies that have looked at it all say it needs treating', was the most common response. I did secure a few, and the clients were appreciative of my honesty, but in the main people felt happier believing whatever the other two or three companies had said. The fact that no one had obviously ever heard of my company was also a major handicap. I had possibly misjudged the situation whilst working for Sprayum and Scarper; by not fully realising that it was much easier to secure contracts under their name as they were an old established company having been in the area for twenty years or so. It was certainly easier getting work in where for example; a floor had completely rotted away and the person could see and understand the problem: or where dampness in the property had caused the plaster to be stained with water with sections of it literally falling off the walls, but these were extreme cases. Stitchum and Cheatum's words on this subject were now foremost in my thoughts. Perhaps they knew what they were talking about after all. It was beginning to make some sort of sense to quote to treat everything, whether or not it was necessary, which all of the companies did of course, and made smaller less well known firms like mine appear incompetent for 'missing' areas. Being a 'Good Samaritan', a phrase one of them used cynically, 'was a complete waste of time' was now coming back to haunt me.

By the end of our first week, Keith and Ben had completed the floor replacement and had hacked off the plaster and installed the new damp course. We now urgently needed a plasterer to go around there and plaster the walls. Most of the plasterers I spoke to were busy. The ones I knew that had worked for Sprayum and Scarper had gone off somewhere in search of work. In the end after numerous phone calls I decided to throw caution to the wind and phone Jon. The reason for this hesitancy was that Jon, although a remarkably good plasterer was unfortunately mentally unstable and prone to violent outbursts at the slightest provocation. He was quite a fearsome looking character being about six feet six with a badly scarred face after having been 'glassed' whilst working as a night club doorman. His eyes were a cold grey colour and were completely emotionless. The most off putting thing about him was without any doubt his voice. Even whilst standing next to you he would shout loudly and aggressively as if in a heated argument. I'd used him before with a great deal of trepidation on vacant properties, but never where the owner was around. Now I had to risk it. Leaving the walls un-plastered at the property for days or possibly weeks on end wasn't an option either for the client or for me as we desperately needed the money in. Trying to take every possible precaution, I called around to the job on the pretext of checking the work out, but really I was trying to establish whether the owner was likely to be there during the day time the following week.   Luckily it seemed that he was going to be working in London for the week and would be away from seven in the morning until seven or eight in the evening. His wife was also going to be away looking after an elderly relative for a few days, which all fitted in perfectly. All we actually needed was two full days which would complete the plastering, and with any luck no one would cross Jon's path. So far so good. I phoned Jon again and after five minutes of him shouting aggressively down the telephone at me, he agreed to do it. At last things seemed to be fitting together. I now had another full week's work for Ben doing the smaller jobs I had booked in, and in a few days time would collect four and a half thousand pounds for the one big job we will have completed.

The enquiries were tailing off noticeably. I'd decided to use at least half the money due to us on Wednesday to place another series of adverts in the local papers which hopefully would generate another flurry of inspections. The idea of spending so much on these was seriously unpalatable: but nonetheless, vitally necessary. I was working on the basic premise that it would make good sense to invest any profits in advertising at least for the first year or so in order to get the new company established. I imagined that after this time the enquiries would come through recommendations from satisfied customers.

The weekend should have been an opportunity to relax and forget about the business. I found this impossible though: I was beginning to feel apprehensive about a number of things which were not immediately discernible. The main worry I suppose, was having to employ the services of Jon the psychotic plasterer.   I was also now beginning to have nagging doubts about the perceived wisdom of my ethical policy. I knew really that a fair proportion of the jobs I had quoted for were being lost simply because of this moralistic stance of trying to 'buck the trend'. I found it immensely frustrating that despite my attempts to provide an honest assessment of whatever the problem might be, people generally preferred to be conned by the larger organisations who were employing Sprayum and Scarper type salesmen working on commission that were of course completely devoid of any scruples.

My uneasiness about Jon stems from an incident that took place a couple of years ago when he was plastering a small extension we were working on. He was experiencing a lot of personal problems at the time after having been released on bail for psychiatric reports following a charge of grievous bodily harm: this followed his unfortunate discovery of his wife in bed with his labourer. What seemed to disturb him most of all about this was the fact that 'Jimmy' the labourer, didn't have the decency to take his boots off before climbing into the marital kip. The client we were working for was standing behind him watching with some fascination, and admiration, the deftness of his plastering strokes. Unfortunately, Jon, obviously preoccupied, didn't realise he was there, turned around and jumped out of his skin. He grabbed the client by the throat and accused him of 'creeping up on him'. The client was absolutely terrified, and quite understandably ran into the house and called the police. Jon reacted violently and uncontrollably when the police arrived and was later sectioned for twenty eight days. That was the last I'd heard of him until my phone call to him a few days ago. He'd assured me that he was 'calmer' now and that was just a difficult phase he was going through.

Mercifully, the next few days passed without any major problems. Further adverts were placed in the newspapers, and the 'permanent' staff members, Gloria and Ben seemed to be enjoying working for The Ethical Preservation Company.

Although the enquiries were coming in at a reasonable rate for a week or so after the adverts came out, there were never enough jobs to justify the cost of this expenditure. Yet without advertising there simply wouldn't be enough enquiries to keep it going. It was becoming increasingly apparent that my ethical stance simply wasn't paying off. By the end of the first month there was virtually nothing in the bank and worse still were the debts of around five thousand pounds. After only four weeks trading it looked very much as if I had reached the end of the road. I knew it would be impossible to borrow any further money from Harry, and even more hopeless trying to arrange an overdraft with the bank. I knew also that even if I could arrange a further loan it would only keep the operation going for another month or two at the most. I now felt quite bitter and disillusioned about trying to run an ethical business. I was quickly learning, and learning the hard way that there is nothing moral or ethical about 'business, or more accurately, this particular business. The naïve amongst us that believe in treating people fairly will surely perish by the wayside.

The most difficult part of all of this was having to explain to Gloria and Ben that I could keep them on until the end of the week but that was it. To my great surprise they were both quite devastated. The following day Gloria came up with a plan. She and Ben had faith in 'effycool preservations' and they both thought that it was worth saving. After a secret discussion they'd had the previous evening they decided they wanted to lend me some money to get over this 'hurdle' as Gloria put it. She was prepared to come up with five thousand pounds, and Ben could do the same. This was something I couldn't have possibly anticipated. Where on earth did they get money from? And even more perplexing, why would they want to put it into what was quite clearly a bottomless pit? I thanked them both for having such faith in this new venture, but explained that I couldn't possibly take their money. Neither of them it would seem, would take no for an answer.

They both enjoyed working for me, and were convinced that our current troubles were just a temporary blip. I knew very well that if I were to take them up on this loan, within a few weeks we would be back to square one with all of our dreams and hopes dashed. The only way I could accept the money would be to change direction on my erstwhile ethical policy. After all it would hardly be ethical to use their money in propping up a ridiculous moral stance that I knew was now doomed to failure. Harry could afford to lose: I didn't feel particularly guilty about losing his money. Gloria and Ben were in a different league. The other problem was the possibility of feeling beholden to them: our employer employee relationship would be affected. Would this actually work?

Whatever the problems might be, the alternative was even more unpleasant. I would never find out if, with this new injection of funds, the business could have been saved or not, and would always be regretting not having taken them up on their kind offer. Only one thing for it, I thanked them both and confirmed that I would try as hard as I could to bring about a change in our fortunes.

As if by magic the next morning Gloria produced a plastic bag stuffed with notes of various denominations, and ten minutes later Ben appeared with an old shoe box with two crocodile clips securing the lid. Inside were bundles of notes with elastic bands wrapped around them. They both confirmed that their respective offerings amounted to exactly five thousand pounds each. There was certainly something quite bizarre if not surreal about the casual way these packages were handed over. Neither Gloria nor Ben were concerned about recording the transaction or discussing any sort of repayment time frame. In fact Ben's only words were 'Good luck, let's hope it helps'. I suspect the person least impressed with this bounty was the cashier at the bank, whose job it was to count it all several times and band it up into the various denominations. The manager: a grey reptilian sort of

137

fellow glanced over at me a couple of times as the money was being counted, sniffed the air around me as if to confirm its putridity and glided off. I suspected there was a secret alarm system under the counter the cashiers used to alert his attention whenever anyone looked as shifty and suspicious as I probably did. I did of course wonder where all this cash came from but didn't allow this to preoccupy my thoughts: there were far too many other things to think about right now. The first imperative was to place some further adverts in the local papers, and pay off the outstanding debts. The adrenalin was now really pumping; this was now a last chance, a serious case of do or die.

That evening I stayed on in the office, bought some greasy fish and chips and a large bottle of white wine and set about designing and planning a new series of adverts. This time the gloves were off, it simply had to work. I decided the ploy I would use would be to guarantee to undercut any legitimate estimate that anyone had received in the last four weeks by at least ten per cent. This way I could be certain of beating all the competition. Morally I was able to justify this in a round about sort of way in that even if the work the other firms had quoted for wasn't all strictly necessary, I would at least be saving them ten per cent. I had already proven beyond any doubt that trying to convince people of my honesty and good intentions was not exactly proving to be very successful.

Chapter Ten

Having now spent nearly half of Gloria and Ben's cash on three large adverts in the local papers, there was really very little to do but sit back and hope. No other enquiries were forthcoming: the telephones were silent apart from the few jackals that tried to sell us a multitude of things from advertising space to photocopiers, and much to my amusement; a debt collection service. Gloria remarked quite astutely that it would be nice if we did have a few debtors.

After five long tortuous days of acute anxiety the adverts came out. The response was quite incredible. Both Gloria and I were answering the phones continuously, booking in appointments, and in many cases booking in the work in advance of the inspection. On the first day of the adverts appearing we'd had twenty two enquiries and four large jobs booked in pending a visit from me and confirmation. I now knew that miraculously I'd hit the right button. I carried out six of the inspections that afternoon, and another four in the evening out of which eight of them were confirmed and booked in.

Realising that the next day there were a further twelve possible jobs to book in, plus a further twenty or God knows how many more that might well arise from this one advert alone, apart from two more that were yet to appear: I telephoned every one I knew in the building trade in an effort to recruit as much labour as I could to try and cope with the massive volume of work that was now coming in. Most of the people I spoke to were still unemployed and were delighted to hear from me despite the fact that half of them were fast asleep at nearly midnight when I'd phoned. The following morning 'effycool preservations' was now seriously operational: we had a workforce of six. Two were carpenters, two were plasterers, one had been working as waiter and the other was Ben. As Ben was the only one who knew anything about timber treatments or damp proofing, they all joined him for a one day crash course in one of the empty properties I had booked in the previous day.

The next problem Gloria and I had was trying to cope with the volume of phone calls coming in which started at seven thirty in the morning. I was now beginning to feel slightly overwhelmed and could detect a certain amount of panic in my own behaviour. I thought about trying to cancel the other two adverts but knew it would be too late: they were both due out today. Somehow or other I managed to inspect the twelve remaining properties we had booked in the day before and immediately booked the work for in four of them. By the end of the day we'd had another twenty six enquiries for the following two days, with just under a third of them booking the work in, again in advance of my visit. At this point we now had the six men booked up for the next six weeks. The jobs were coming in faster than I could cope with and we desperately needed more of everything. I bought two more second hand desks and word processors for our tiny office, and Gloria persuaded two of her friends who were both equally well proportioned, to come in and bash the reports and estimates out. Having run out of contacts now in the building trade; I advertised for more skilled people including general operatives, carpenters, plasterers and estimators. The work just kept coming in and the money kept going out even faster.

Up until now I hadn't given a moments thought to Grimshaw my friendly old bank manager. I was however unpleasantly reminded of him when a letter arrived explaining that the bank was applying to the courts for an order to repossess my house to recover the monies it had lent to my previous building business. The monies that Gloria and Ben had loaned me had rapidly been absorbed in wages and numerous other costs which meant we were really back to square one, except this time things were very different, weren't they?

Feeling more confident now, I decided the best plan would be to go see Grimshaw face to face and explain how things had progressed. This wasn't a decision arrived at easily as I had been harbouring extremely sinister thoughts of which would be the slowest and most painful way to terminate his exposure for the long term. Knowing what banks were like, I had already prepared a cash flow forecast based on the massive turn around on the prospects of Ethical Preservation which showed quite clearly that by a strange quirk of luck, that I had now hit the jackpot. Certainly within three months I would be able to pay off all the outstanding loans secured against my house: all I needed now as a matter of urgency was an immediate short term injection of about ten thousand pounds. Unfortunately, Grimshaw didn't seem to share my optimism. What offended him most of all apparently, was the fact that I was using another bank: Harry's bank. 'Had you of come to me in the first place we would have carefully looked at your proposal and I dare say would have been prepared to assist you', he said. I tried to stay reasonably calm whilst reminding him that he'd basically pulled the plug on the building company I'd had before. If the bank would have been prepared to assist me, why did they do this then? 'I think the answer to that question' he said, is that we wrote to you suggesting you 'furnish' us with a 'constructive methodology' to reduce the banks exposure in the light of the current economic downturn, and we failed to receive a satisfactory response from you. Under the circumstances you gave us little choice'. 'Bollocks' I shouted, got up, slammed the door and walked out. Whilst walking back to my car in a

141

murderous frame of mind I was measurably consoled by thinking of the comment of Mark Twain, that a bank manager is someone that will lend you an umbrella when the sun is shining, but demands it back when it starts to rain.

I still, nonetheless, felt very angry that I had misjudged the situation and moreover wasted valuable time on this exercise. I also now had to think quickly and scheme up another way to raise some urgently needed additional capital to tide us over for the next few weeks. It now perversely seemed that my sudden good fortune with getting all this work in was now actually forcing the business into insolvency. If I were to approach the bank I am using now: Harry's bank, they would definitely draw a blank without his further involvement and participation. It would also sour my relationship with him somewhat if the bank contacted him, which they surely would, explaining that I was trying to borrow money in a business that he now owned twenty five per cent of. Only one thing for it, I thought, I must speak to him: Explain how things had developed, and being a shrewd operator, he would hopefully come up with a further ten thousand.

Again, I had badly misjudged human nature. Harry was delighted that work had picked up and that the business was taking off with a vengeance. He ran through my figures and confirmed that this 'looked like a winner' using his phraseology. Yes, he would be happy to invest a further ten thousand pounds on the same basis as before: All he wanted for this was a further twenty five per cent of the shares, giving him a total of fifty per cent. I laughed; feeling enormously relieved knowing that he was joking about owning another quarter of the business. I then realised he wasn't.

I had absolutely no idea where or how Gloria or Ben had acquired the cash they had lent me, and to be quite honest I didn't really want to know. Was it remotely possible they had access to more of it? Under normal circumstances I wouldn't have dreamed of asking them if they could find anymore: but these were far from normal circumstances. It was now midday on Friday: Wages were due in a few hours time, something had to happen. Nothing else for it, I drove back to the office which was buzzing with life. Gloria was booking in even more inspections and her two friends were hammering away on the word processors at an alarming speed. I couldn't speak to Gloria with the other two women there, and I obviously couldn't ask them to leave our one roomed office for ten minutes. I decided the only safe route through would be for me to go out to a public phone box, call in and explain the position to her.

"Good Morning, this is 'effycool preservations' Gloria speaking, how can I help you?

"Gloria, this is Clive, I hate to ask you this, but we've got a slight problem."

"Wos happened? Where are you?"

"Outside the office, in the phone box, I couldn't talk to you in the office, and it's a bit urgent. The meeting with the bank didn't go very well. I went on to see Harry, and that didn't go very well either."

"Bastards," she said. "They're all the same these people with money, they'll never give you nuffink unless you're rolling in money and don't need it. How much do you need?"

"Well, I was trying to borrow another ten thousand, it's perfectly safe for them, the work's coming in . . .things couldn't be better, but as you say, it seems they'll only lend it to you if don't really need it anyway."

"Don't worry Clive, I'm going home for half an hour at lunch time, I'll bring it back with me this afternoon."

"What do you mean?"

"The ten grand, I'll bring it back with me after lunch."
Feeling almost speechless, I managed to say 'thanks' and hung up.

The morning's abortive visits to the bank and Harry meant that I was way behind with the inspections that were booked. I now had move around like a maniac to try and keep ahead of this continuous flow of appointments. I left a note on Gloria's desk thanking her for the further loan and asked her if she would pay it into the bank.

By nine thirty that evening I had completed sixteen inspections: booked in more work for operatives that I hadn't yet employed, and at two o'clock on Saturday morning had finally drafted out the reports and estimates. The following day, Saturday, which had already started; there were another twelve inspections booked. This time they were all over the place with twenty or thirty miles between one address and the next. Sunday was spent drafting out more estimates, this would leave Monday morning free to interview more people including more carpenters and plasterers. I also placed another advert for estimators and building surveyors, as it had now become blatantly evident that I would not be able to continue working at this rate for very much longer. I really was wondering if I had bitten off more than I could chew. I had never remotely anticipated the sort of success that seemed to be magically taking place, and felt a strange sort of ambivalence about it. I really wasn't trying to make a fortune, nor did I want to be tied to the continual stress and pressure of running a rapidly expanding trading company. My building company before was a very laid back affair: we were really just a group of old pals working together at a leisurely pace, and drawing enough to live on each week. One job always seemed to follow another.

I was becoming increasingly aware that having now resolved the immediate cash flow problems, certain moves would have to be made. We urgently needed a bigger office, an up to date telephone system, decent office furniture, and at least five more fully equipped vans. I had worked out that we currently had nearly twelve weeks work booked ahead for six men and a similar amount of work that we hadn't yet booked in.

On Monday I employed a further six operatives, and two estimators. The new vans were acquired on a contract hire basis and were being sign written. At the back of my mind was a constant haunting fear that if the enquiries stopped coming in now the whole enterprise would collapse very quickly like a pack of cards. Somehow though, I managed not to dwell on this prospect and thought it would be wise to use the rest of the afternoon searching for a new office: somewhere ideally close by, where we could become properly organised without actually sitting on top of each other. Unfortunately this necessitated a visit to the offices of Vileman and Leech, the local agents dealing in commercial premises. The most interesting premises they had on their books was a disused bank, directly opposite Sprayum and Scarpers office, and next door to an off licence. This seemed to fit the bill in every respect. The premises had an enormous ground floor area with a built in safe and strong room; upstairs there were four large rooms, a kitchen and bathroom. Behind the bank was a rear entrance with four parking spaces. This was too good to turn down. With a little bartering and negotiating with the reptilian Vileman and the landlords, I obtained a fifty per cent reduction in the first quarters rent provided that I signed a new seven year lease. This was terrific; I rushed back to give Gloria the good news and found the office being 'turned over'. The girls looked terrified; they were ashen white and were huddled in the tiny kitchen area whilst four thuggish looking individuals were pulling the place apart. All the drawers had been pulled out of the desks; the desks were upside down on the floor: the carpet had been ripped up and floorboards yanked up all over the room.

"What the hell's going on?" I shouted.

"Who are you?" one of them shouted at me aggressively.

"What the hell's that got to do with you? What on earth do you think you're doing?"

The first one of them I spoke to stood up poked a card in a leather holder right in front of my face and said "We're police officers and we're carrying out a search of these premises. I presume you are the owner of these premises is that correct?"

Feeling completely dumfounded all I could say was "Yes."

"We have good reason to believe that a very serious offence has been committed and we have a warrant to search these premises. It will be in your interests to cooperate with us. We will be as quick as we can but I must advise you that any attempt by yourself or others to impede, obstruct, or otherwise interfere with this process, could result in you being arrested and removed from the premises. Do you understand what I am saying to you?"

"Well yes of course, but what sort of offence are you talking about?"

"I am afraid I'm not at liberty to disclose that information. I can tell you that our search is just about completed and I need to ask you some questions."

"Right." I said, "fire away."

"You have a Ben Carter working for you: where is he working right now?"

"Ben? Well, he's carrying out some work in a client's house spraying the roof timbers for woodworm."

"Give me the address."

"Why what's he done?"

"I've already explained that I am not at liberty to divulge this information to you, all I can say is that we believe he has committed a very serious offence."

"I'm sorry." I said. "I'm trying to run a business here. If you're not going to tell me what you want him for; I'm not going to tell you where he's working. Arrest me if you want to, I don't care."

That seemed to soften his aggressive attitude a little.

"Well we have evidence to prove that he's been dealing in class 'A' drugs."

"O.K," I said, I'm sorry to hear that. Is that what you're looking for here: drugs?"

"Yes it is. Now would you be kind enough to let us have the address of where he is working?"

"Look, if I give you this, It's fairly obvious that you're going to rush in there, arrest Ben in front of the client and I dare say pull their house apart just as you've done here. That sort of publicity would mean the end of my business"

"No sir, no, no, no, I can assure you all we will do is wait discretely somewhere near the property and approach him when he leaves. I am a patient man but I am not prepared to wait any longer for this information. I will ask you one more time, if you fail to cooperate with us you will be arrested now and will possibly be charged with obstructing the police in the course of their duty."

On that basis, I gave him the address. They all then picked up the various tools, torches, and other implements that were scattered about and rushed out of the office leaving us to reinstate everything. Half an hour later we had the client at Ben's job screaming hysterically down the telephone. The police had evidently forced their way into her house, wrestled Ben to the floor as he was leaving, and quite understandably had terrified the life out of her. Gloria attempted to calm her, whilst I drove straight round there in order to try and contain the situation. I still had absolutely no idea of the extent of Ben's involvement in the supposed drug dealing charge, but managed after nearly two hours to convince her that the police were after him for non payment of parking fines. I phoned Ben's number continuously throughout the evening and no one answered. I then decided to call round to the local police station to try and find out what was happening. Evidently he was being held in custody pending further searches of his house, his parent's house, and other properties where friends of his could be hiding stashes of drugs for him. The following day he was released on bail after having been charged with supplying a 'small' amount of cannabis. According to him it was about two ounces. Had he of been involved in an armed robbery or kidnap and murder, I really don't think the reaction of the policemen involved in this could have been any more melodramatic. I did now of course have an idea of where his cash came from.

Things were now moving at an alarming rate. We now had a work force of twelve men; most of them had their own tools and vans which took some of the pressure off as far as transport was concerned. In another week the five new vans would be on the road all freshly sign written and looking the part. One of the estimators I had agreed to employ had evidently died of a heart attack the night before he was due to start: surely the prospect of working for Ethical Preservation wasn't that frightening. Not exactly a good omen. The other one, a very serious looking fellow called Brian, had started, and seemed to know what he was doing. Under normal circumstances I would have spent a few days with him, but now had to trust to luck that it would work out. I had roughly worked out that if he didn't secure at least sixty per cent of the enquiries he went after, particularly as we were undercutting everyone else, then we would part fairly rapidly, but thankfully he performed extremely well. Brian's physiognomy wasn't really one of his greatest attributes: Although he was pleasantly spoken and presentable, his face had certain rat like features about it: A constant quivering and twitching of the nostrils and lower lip. I concluded this must have developed from years of sniffing around people's houses trying to work out much he could extract from them. The fact that he wasn't allowed into the office: purely on the grounds that there was nowhere for him so sit, didn't seem to worry him too much. I did explain that we were about to 'take over' a bank, and he would then have a suitable place to sit at. So for the time being he seemed happy enough using his car outside to sit in and write up the various reports.

In order to keep the vital cash flow going either Brian or I would call around to each job in the evening after it was completed and present the client with an invoice. Virtually all of them paid up on the spot. I certainly didn't enjoy having to do this but it would have been foolish and naive to assume that they would pay up quickly without any prompting.

Although the enquiries were still coming in, the flow was reduced somewhat, so I decided to place a further series of large adverts the local papers again. This time they appeared alongside similar adverts from Sprayum and Scarper and a few others, all much along the same lines as my first set of adverts offering to better any estimate: this time by fifteen per cent in the case of Sprayum and Scarper, and by twenty per cent by some of the others. I realised instantly that now some other ploy was needed. The response we got this time was predictably muted: Not that it particularly mattered right now as we had enough work for the next three months, but it was certainly something to think about.

The day we were to move into our new office coincided with the court hearing from Grimshaw to repossess my house. I decided to attend the hearing and contest their application on the grounds that they over reacted in withdrawing my overdraft, thereby preventing my perfectly sound building company from trading. I was quite confident that the judge would take into account my current good fortune with the Ethical Preservation business and block their request. I sacrificed any sleep the night before, drafting out a cash flow forecast showing the quite incredible profits that would be generated by the new business and that I would easily be able to pay these loans off within the next twelve months. I had no doubt that this would do the trick and would give me a little more breathing space.

I was wrong.

The judge didn't really appear too interested in me, or what I had to say. He seemed to be totally sympathetic to the little tubercular looking weasel in a red waistcoat that Grimshaw had sent to represent the bank. Before I'd actually had a chance to properly present my case; the order was made. The most sickening and frustrating thing about this was that I could have, at a push, have paid all of Grimshaw's loans off in three months time. Right now, I knew it would be impossible to borrow any more money, and felt quite impotent. In many ways, finding our new office was a godsend. I could now as a temporary measure, move into the rooms above and have some sort of security until the new business was properly established. Trying to look on the bright side; I'd worked out that there would be enough equity from the sale of my house to pay off the bank, and clear the loans from Gloria and Ben. With any luck, this would also leave some money over for emergency funding if things were to take a downward turn on the work front.

Within a couple of hours we managed to move the battered old furniture and bits of second hand office equipment we had into the ground floor of the bank. There was something quite bizarre and surreal about this. The first impression when entering through the massive hardwood doors was something akin to a world war one recruiting depot and a Romanian refugee centre. The main area was about six metres by eight metres with two small partitioned rooms to the rear with a small kitchen and toilet area. I decided that Brian could use one of these rooms and I would commandeer the other. I couldn't help wondering how many people had sat nervously in these rooms in front of the Grimshaw's of this world, having their hopes dashed and in some cases their lives ruined by the callous greedy ethos that is endemic in the banking industry.

After adapting to our vastly contrasting change of surroundings the business now seemed to have taken on a feeling of solidity and permanence. My plan to replace our tatty office furniture and upgrade all the equipment was going to have to wait until I had repaid Gloria and Ben. If things worked out; I would also have liked to have repaid Harry; and at the same time come up with an offer which might tempt him to relinquish his twenty five per cent stake in the business. The most important thing to concentrate on right now was making sure that the jobs were completed on time without any problems.   Knowing the attitude of the banks to small businesses, I knew that however profitable the business looked, or in fact, was; their attitude wasn't going to change. As far as they were concerned, we were now in a recession and any small business was doomed to failure. If they saw any opportunity to precipitate this they would jump at it.

We had been in our new office for just over four weeks with everything running reasonably smoothly until the police arrived and took Gloria away. I was out carrying out inspections at the time: when I returned to the office, the other two girls Carol and Brenda were almost hysterical. Evidently the police had told them that they would be questioned later as part of their on going investigation. I asked them what it was all about but realised they weren't going to tell me. I drove to the local police station to try and find out what was going on. I assumed that she might have been assisting Ben in some way, but really had no idea. At the police station I was told that she was still being interviewed in respect of a very serious matter, and she would probably be released later on that afternoon.

This completely unexpected development convinced me that there was some sort of conspiracy working against us. Gloria was now the king pin of the whole enterprise. Was this something hatched by Sprayum and Scarper? Perhaps this was all part of some evil plan that Grimshaw had concocted.

Just before six o'clock when the office was about to close, Gloria appeared looking slightly apprehensive, but was otherwise her normal cheery self.

"Sorry about all this Clive." She said. "I've run into a slight bit of 'bovver' with the 'ole bill' if you know what I mean."

It turned out that Gloria's flat was above 'Blue Heaven', the local lap dancing club. The police had received reports from neighbours that men had been seen leaving the club in the early hours and were going straight from there, up to her flat. According to Gloria, it was just a party with her and her friends. The police obviously had other ideas and were, it seemed, now deciding what further action to take. I of course, now understood how it was Gloria was able to find all the cash to inject into my ailing enterprise.

Although I did feel sorry for her, I couldn't restrain guffaws of laughter when it suddenly dawned on me that my ethical preservation business was being financed from the proceeds of tax evasion, drug dealing and prostitution.

Although the police did interview Brenda and Carol, for some reason they decided to take no further action. I did suspect that this may well have been because they were using the club themselves together with the after hours services provided by the girls above.

I never really understood why it was, but the business continued to prosper. Every few weeks I would dream up some 'spectacular' offer to attract more enquiries, which included a whole gamut of gimmicks from free colour televisions, to free holidays. None of these were free of course; anything that was offered was added to the price of the job: but amazingly it worked. After being established for only eight months, we now had sixteen full time operatives and a total of eight fully equipped vans. We also had a separate plastering division, along with four estimators, and a contracts manager who organised the jobs and the workforce. My house had been repossessed by the bank, and I was now living in the rooms above our office. Initially this did seem like a good idea, but as the work force expanded, it became blatantly evident that these rooms were urgently needed to accommodate the extra office employees. I'd started off using the whole first floor area, and very quickly my domestic paraphernalia had to be condensed into three rooms, then two, and finally one: with everything piled up around the room with just enough space for me to get to the bed. I had now repaid the outstanding loans to Gloria and Ben and had given them both a generous 'bonus' for their support. Although apart from losing my house, I knew I should have felt ecstatic at the amazing success of this venture: but in truth I was beginning to realise that being a 'businessman' wasn't for me. I was now playing and acting out a role which was totally alien to me. Everything now was organised in such a way that apart from overseeing the operation, I had little part in the actual day to day running of this money making machine. I enjoyed working physically, but knew that now this would have been completely incongruous and out of the question. I thought about TM and Andrew at Sprayum and Scarper, and how much I hated and despised everything they stood for. I'd always had a pathological loathing for these kinds of people, and now I was becoming like them. I felt I had created some sort of evil greedy monster with an appetite that could never be satiated. There was no work satisfaction, just a frantic repetitive continuum of meaningless enquiries, estimates, jobs, invoices, and so on . . . feeding the hungry mouth of the beast. Not long after reaching these conclusions I learnt that Sprayum and Scarper were in liquidation. According to the newspaper article, this had been caused by increased competition in the industry, and a severe downturn in the economy resulting in their bank 'finding it impossible to offer them further support'. At first I felt overjoyed . . . euphoric even: I then felt slight pangs of guilt, knowing that I had probably contributed to their demise. This also reinforced my belief that there can never be any peace of mind or security when a bank has its slimy grasping tentacles around a business whether it is large or small.

A few weeks after this I was glancing through our inspection enquiry sheets for the following day and saw my address, or to be absolutely correct; the address of my house that the bank had snatched from me. The sale of the property was being auctioned by Floggum and Smarmy in three days time. I quickly grabbed a bank statement from Ethical Preservation and checked the balance. I then worked out a rough cash summary and could see that there was more than enough cash in the business for me to buy it.

153

Three days later, the auctioneers gavel gave a resounding crack on the hardwood lectern in front of him which was followed by 'Sold to Mr West'. This felt rather like a strange dream: I wondered if I had now lost touch with reality. Something I hadn't taken into account was the fact that even after the bank had taken the outstanding loans and their 'costs' out of the sale proceeds, they would still have to return more than half of the amount realised back to me which was mine. One thing was quite certain: as soon as I moved back into the house I would have a serious house warming party with a special invitation being sent to Grimshaw. Being back in my own house again, without being beholden to anyone; caused me to reflect yet again on my own motivation. The years I spent living here running and working in my small relaxed building firm with a few old friends were without doubt very happy times. The only real stress I experienced was caused by Grimshaw: now that he no longer featured in my future, I wondered if it would be possible to return to those relaxed carefree times. Money, power or wealth was, or never had been a goal for me: I still had the same old car that I'd bought more than six years ago. I was now beginning to see the light. Doubtless, losing my building firm had shaken my stability and undeniable complacence. Nearly losing the new company after only a few weeks of trading had prompted me to overreact, which perversely, was resulting in me beating Sprayum and Scarper and all the other villains in the business at their own game.

Chapter Eleven

As the weeks sped by, the paperwork and financial record keeping increased to such an extent that Gloria, although trying her best to attend to everything was now becoming swamped with an ever increasing amount of bookkeeping. My accountant suggested that as the business had expanded so quickly we now needed a full time bookkeeper and financial controller to carry out these functions and to ensure that the finances of the company were kept on an even keel. For me, the prospect of this was not particularly appealing. Would I have to ask this persons permission before I bought new office equipment, a new van, a box of paperclips or anything else for that matter? Although cash flow hadn't been a recent problem; the fact that things could rapidly change overnight was a thought that constantly haunted me. Now that I had vacated 'my room' upstairs at the office, this, I decided, would be a suitable place for him to work. All that was needed was to place an advert in the local paper and interview the prospective candidates. It was agreed that when the replies came in the following week, Gloria would arrange for any suitable applicants to be interviewed. The first one I interviewed was a shifty alcoholic looking accountant who confessed that he had just been released after serving a three year prison term for embezzlement. He assured me that he was now a completely reformed character and just wanted another chance. Another chance at what? I thought.

It was really quite impossible to determine the gender of the second applicant: A fairly well built person dressed in a pin stripe suit with a high pitched squeaky voice and sporting violet coloured nail varnish. 'His' name was Charles: He had evidently been employed by a large women's fashion warehouse and was lamenting the fact that they were now in receivership. Having curtailed this interview fairly swiftly, I now had twenty minutes before the next applicant was due to arrive. I sat for a while day staring out of my cubicle, dreaming really. I had a strong feeling of alienation and detachment: my heart began pounding away at a speed I was unaccustomed to; beads of sweat were trickling down my face. What on earth was I doing here? Whatever it was, I no longer wanted to be part of it: I felt as if I was playing a part in a weird play of some kind. Perhaps the stress of the past year or so was now catching up with me. Perhaps everything had happened so quickly that I now needed time to adjust. Could it be that I was losing touch with reality? Is this what people experience before they have nervous breakdowns?

I looked at my watch and glanced down at the diary to check the next appointment time again. 3.30pm 'Reginald Grimshaw'. Grimshaw? I started: Must be Gloria playing a joke on me. I got up and opened the door of my little partitioned office and shouted across to Gloria,

"Very funny Gloria; this 3.30 appointment; it actually made me jump when I looked at it."

Gloria stopped typing gave a half smile and looked at me with a mystified expression.

"What do you mean?" she said.

"Grimshaw: I do like your sense of humour."

"Sorry Clive, I don't understand."

"Grimshaw, the name in the diary . . . my obnoxious bank manager is expecting to work here with us, yes that really is very funny."

Before Gloria could say anymore, the large oak door was flung open and there he was: Grimshaw . . . standing there grinning sheepishly.

My first suspicions were probably correct: I was in fact losing touch with reality. How could this person possibly be Grimshaw? I took half a step backwards and pressed the point of a pen I was holding into my thumb, yes, I could feel the pain of it as my skin was punctured. This wasn't a dream. Bright red spots of blood appeared on the carpet like large drops of rain. I then took a few steps forward towards him. Yes it was quite definitely him. I wasn't imagining it: this was really happening.

"Hello I have an appointment to see a Mr West," he said whilst extending a damp flabby bank managers hand forward for me to shake.

Being taken aback, and without thinking I held out my blood soaked hand and then withdrew it. Gloria, who was seated in front of us stopped typing and handed me some tissues.

"Struth, what have you done?" she said.

"It's nothing," I replied and wrapped the tissues around my punctured thumb.

Grimshaw took half a step forward as if to assist and then stopped as if frozen to the spot.

"That looks quite nasty perhaps you ought to run up to the hospital to get it seen to," he said.

"My car is right outside; I'll drive you up there if you like."

I ignored this and stared at him. "What are you doing here?" I asked.

"As I said, I've arranged an appointment to see a Mr West . . .Oh . . .Oh dear, I simply didn't occur to me: It's you is it? Oh I am sorry; I just didn't put two and two together. Had the advertisement said contact Mr Clive West, I suspect it would have jogged my memory; I then might have realised that you were one of the bank's old customers."

"Better come into my office," I said to him, deciding that some protracted form of explanation was about to be proffered as to his presence here seeking employment.

"It's strange for me being in here," he said. "I started off my banking career over thirty years ago at this branch."

"Are you no longer working for the bank?" I asked him.

"Well, you may well know about the takeover," he said, looking at me expecting some sort of affirmative response.

"Well, maybe not," he continued, realising that there was no reaction from me and that I was just waiting impatiently for him to come out with whatever it was he was about to divulge.

"Well, as I was about to explain, the 'Snatchemall Banking Corporation' took over our bank a few months ago, and as part of that takeover they were looking to reduce costs which unfortunately resulted in some redundancies."

"I've got it," I said gleefully. "So you've been made redundant?"

"Well not exactly, let's say that I elected to accept early retirement. The package they offered me was quite generous, so I decided that this might be the right time to explore other possibilities."

"I understand; so you want a job?" I said scathingly.

"Look, I do hope there's no bad feeling between us," he said pathetically.

"Why on earth should you think that?" I questioned.

"Well, sometimes some of the decisions we have to make as bank managers aren't necessarily popular ones, or for that matter the personal choice of the individual manager; it's more to do with carrying out the bank's policy with regard to its own often difficult and sometimes rigid lending criteria."

"I would prefer to forget about what happened: I'm trying hard to rebuild my life," I said. "I have bought my house back, and as you well know I have started another business. I've been able to do this without any help from banks, or should I say more precisely . . . from you. Had I relied on the

158

wisdom and generosity of banks, I would now be unemployed, on the street, and most probably starving."

I could feel myself becoming more and more annoyed simply by his fat contented and unctuous presence. Here sitting a couple of feet away was the cause of so much stress, pain, insecurity and the murderous feelings that I was still trying desperately to overcome. I reflected quickly upon a saying of Oscar Wilde; 'you should always forgive your enemies: There is nothing that annoys them more': but forgiveness would not come easily seeing this reptilian specimen without shame or humility in front of me.

"Yes, I do understand how you feel, of course its only natural: but the point I'm trying to get across to you is that there really was nothing personal in the decisions that were made. The banks generally, would bend over backwards to prevent a small business like yours from going under, particularly if this meant you losing your house as well. But at the end of the day the shareholders must be protected. I wish things could have been different for both of us, but that's the way it works I'm afraid."

All my self control was now being incorporated in a mammoth effort to prevent me leaping over the desk between us and throttling him. I somehow restrained myself and very quietly and very slowly explained again that I had no wish to discuss this matter any further with him.

"Forgive me, but do you mean that you are not prepared to consider my application for the post you are offering?"

Strangely enough, I considered there might be a satisfying outcome to this situation after all. What if I were to employ him? Revenge after all is a dish best served cold. The possibilities were endless. Instead of one sudden burst of fury and anger, I could torture him slowly with a more subtle approach. What could possibly be more satisfying?

"Are you alright?" he asked.

"Yes, yes, sorry, I was thinking about something," I said, having been completely preoccupied for the last sixty seconds or so with thoughts of him lying on a medieval rack in the basement of my house. Lucky he's not a mind reader I thought. I quickly tried to catch the last threads of our conversation.

"Do bank managers actually know anything about the day to day running of a small business?" I enquired patronisingly.

"Of course they do. Managing the branch of a bank is in effect running a small business. On top of that one has to account to the powers that be: you know: everything has to be run in an orderly manner. On top of that you, as the manager of a bank, are responsible in many ways for the whims and extravagancies of thousands of your account holders. One has to have all the qualities of an accountant, a social worker, a debt collector and at times just be a friendly shoulder for them to cry on."

"When you call in their overdrafts do you mean?"

"No, most people think they are living within their means, but in reality most people are in debt: either overdrawn for no good reason, and often without the banks permission, or wondering where the next mortgage payment is going to come from. Many people have debts on credit cards which they will probably never be able to pay off. If you try to explain that they should put their affairs in order they bitterly resent it. Controlling finances is not an easy matter. In a small business like yours it's absolutely essential to introduce strict controls on everything if the business is to survive the unpredictable ups and downs of the market place."

Of course what he was saying did make sense. But somehow the very idea of him hovering around the office casting his beady eyes over everything was distasteful in the ultimate extreme. We undoubtedly needed somebody . . . but surely not him. I decided I must have time to think: I must, I thought, terminate this interview and send him on his way before the overwhelming urge to attack him resurfaced.

"Let me think about it," I said

"Yes of course," he agreed. "I think that would be very wise under the circumstances. Just before I go though, I must just explain very briefly how my own personal situation has changed which might allow you to understand a little more clearly why I am now looking for another position."

"Well, yes it did cross my mind." I mused. "I don't know how old you are, but without any disrespect, you must be fairly close to retirement age anyway: and I presume your house is now paid for and that you will have left the bank with a substantial pension."

"Yes, this is all true. Although I suspected that I might shall we say be 'put out to grass' when the takeover happened, it was nonetheless a shock when it actually happened. I'd always imagined that when I did eventually retire I would have more time to spend on my trains and . . ."

"Sorry . . . what do you mean: your trains?"

"Yes, my trains: Hilda and I have had the roof of our house extended to accommodate the entire track that I have collected over the years. Model railways: it's a hobby of mine you see: an interest, a form of relaxation. Anyway as I was saying, I thought I would be happy to spend more time with this; the occasional spot of fishing, and that Hilda and I would obviously spend more time together: you know going out for drives in the country, afternoon teas, and the odd weekend away where model railway exhibitions and displays were being held, but unfortunately this is not to be."

"Why? What's happened?"

"Well unfortunately Hilda's left me."

"Oh, I'm sorry. Where's she gone?"

"Well I'm afraid to say she ran off the day I received my redundancy package, with her personal trainer."

"Personal trainer? Are you serious?"

Grimshaw's eyes were bulging, and filling with tears. "Yes, I couldn't believe it either," he snuffled.

"I'm sorry to hear it." I said, wondering how it was possible for me to feel anything other than loathing for this dejected ogre of doom.

"The problems go back over many years: Hilda was suffering from a few problems when we first met."

"Problems? What do you mean?"

"Well it used to be called manic depression, but it's commonly known as bipolar disorder now. She'd always, I thought, managed to control it with drugs... you know maintain some sort of equilibrium. Her mood changes though were constantly fluctuating from the manic stage to the depressive stage. Although I realised it must have been incredibly difficult for her to cope with her depression: it was something I had learned somehow to cope with over the years. What I found virtually impossible to deal with were the manic phases."

"Why, what did she do?" I was now becoming intrigued to know more.

"Well it can take many forms, but in her case she spent money: you know just bought things."

"What things? What things are you talking about?"

"Well, anything . . . clothes, perfume, shoes, presents for me, presents for anyone she knew. She would just spend, spend and spend for days on end until the shops closed or until another side of her illness took over."

"Forgive me for asking, but where did she get the money from?"

"No, that's a good question. This was all done with personal loans, store cards and God knows how many credit cards. I'm only now discovering the true extent of her spending sprees."

"God that must be particularly difficult for you: bearing in mind your natural prudence if you know what I mean."

"It's actually far more difficult and far more serious than I could have possibly anticipated. I used to leave the house in the morning before the postman's delivery, which obviously

162

allowed her to gather up all the statements and pay the minimum amount on all the cards that were charged up to their limits, and somehow keep a lid on things. Since she left, I have been opening everything and just couldn't believe the sums involved. I now, I think, know the full amount that she had borrowed which, being married; we are obviously both responsible for."

"How much is it? That is of course if you don't mind my asking."

"Oh let's just say that I now have no other choice than to sell our house to pay off all the outstanding debts. My solicitor has put in place various measures that will ensure that any further debts she runs up will not be my responsibility. During the past few weeks I have seriously wondered if it's worth going on, but I've always been a strong person, and I know that things can't really get any worse. The other evening I was sitting wondering what to do: I'd almost given up hope when I came across your advert and thought 'that's it', get a hold of yourself Reginald, find yourself another job . . .that'll take your mind of things."

This was definitely some form of emotional blackmail. If he leaves here now and decides to jump under a train . . . a real train that is, then I would feel guilty forever. 'Bastard' I thought why's he doing this to me? Am I now to be stuck with this pitiful swine for the rest of my life? I simply couldn't now just turn him down. I'd heard enough though: I looked at my watch and gasped. 'Oh dear I'm late for an appointment'. Grimshaw lifted his plump body out of the chair and apologised for keeping me.

"Mr Grimshaw, I'm sorry to hear your story," I said. "Leave it with me, I need to think it over and I will be in touch with you in a few days."

"I understand, but it's 'Reginald' now please." He proffered the damp flabby hand once more: I stared at it; held out my right hand which was now a congealed bloodied mess; immediately withdrew it and made a sort of grunting sound.

"You must get that looked at," he said, turned around and floated out of the door.

That night, despite copious amounts of white wine, cans of beer and the remnants of a bottle of vodka: sleep eluded me. Every time I closed my eyes I had a vision of Grimshaw bawling his eyes out whilst trying to play with his train set. At one point I did nod off for a few moments but then awoke with a start just as he was about to fling himself under a train. I had other strange visions of Hilda appearing as a terrifying looking femme fatale, scantily clad and covered in gold jewellery; grinning insanely whilst examining the attributes of her personal trainer. Why had this wretched Grimshaw reappeared? This whole saga reminded me of some sort of Faustian nightmare. As the dawn broke I decided the best thing to do now would be to speak to my accountant . . .take his advice. If I were to employ Grimshaw and for whatever reason it didn't work out, at least my conscience would be appeased: I would be exonerated from any further guilt even if he then decided to explore the underneath of a train.

It was still only seven thirty. I had been up now for over an hour: had washed, dressed, had breakfast and started pacing up and down the hallway. Too early yet to go to the office: perhaps a brisk walk along the seafront in the biting chill of this February morning might invigorate the senses I thought. I was surprised to see so many people out at this time in the morning. There were joggers, cyclists, people exercising dogs, some people practising some weird form of martial art, and an amazing number of dishevelled, hopeless looking men standing on the promenade staring blankly into the grey turbulent sea. I wondered how many of them had spent the night down here huddled in the freezing cold on one of the benches inside the fading decadent seaside pavilions that were really now only grim relics of a previous century. How many of these sad and pathetic creatures I wondered, once had busy successful lives: detached houses in 'nice' roads filled with reproduction furniture, hostess trolleys and shag pile carpets, businesses with smart secretaries, top of the range executive cars, and well spoken children with polished faces, exotic foreign holidays twice a year and all the other indicators of a middle class lifestyle. What were they thinking about now? The past? Perhaps how things used to be. I couldn't help thinking there but for the grace of God etc, and then stood by the promenade railing myself: gazed into the cold grey hostile relentless crashing waves and considered just how close I had been to becoming yet another of these God forsaken casualties in our greedy cut throat system of survival of the fittest and winner takes all. I perversely started laughing uncontrollably: I imagined that many of these homeless, starving men were probably once bank managers with wives like Hilda. How unjust it was that although she might have been mentally ill . . . perhaps insane even: but she would not be the one to suffer; you never saw any women down here sleeping on benches: were they not destined some of them to suffer a similar fate? I suspect they were given some almighty exemption from this sort of divine retribution, it would only be Grimshaw down here with all the others staring into the sea.

When I arrived at the office, I'd already decided to make every effort to put the past behind me at least give the fellow a chance. I picked up the phone and dialled his number.

"Good Morning, this is Reginald Grimshaw speaking."

"Ah hello Mr Grimshaw this is Clive West."

"Yes, hello Mr West, it's nice to hear from you."

"Look, I've been thinking things over, and what I suggest if it's acceptable to you, is that you start on a trial basis say four weeks, something like that: if we deal with it this way it will give us both a chance to see if things work out. I don't know how you feel about that, perhaps you'd like to give it some thought and come back to me."

"Yes, I don't need to think about it; that would be perfectly acceptable with me, and a very sensible way to go about things if I may say so."

"Right, that's one thing sorted out: the next thing we need to talk about out is salary."

"Well, I'm quite happy to leave that up to you." Grimshaw said. "If you pay me what you think the job is worth for the initial period; if we are both happy after that we can talk about it again. As I explained, money isn't my prime motivator right at the moment, for me it's more to do with trying to keep occupied, you know . . . having something else to think about."

"Yes I understand," I said. "Well the only other thing is when would you like to start?"

"Well, I'm not doing anything important at the moment, so right away if that's alright with you; say tomorrow morning?"

"Yes, that's fine Mr Grimshaw; we'll look forward to seeing you then."

"Good, excellent, and thank you for giving me this opportunity... you won't regret it I promise. Oh, just one last thing, it's 'Reginald' now."

"Ok Reginald, thanks and goodbye."

Oh my God. What have I done? I asked myself. It might be admirable attempting to adopt a Christian philosophy and be philanthropic; but . . . hell . . .Grimshaw of all people. What the devil's going on? What's happening to me? Grimshaw, the dreaded Grimshaw here . . . working here . . . perhaps it's not just his wife that needs help. What on earth was I thinking of? Oh bugger it, it's done now: too late to stop it. I suppose at worst it could last for four weeks, after that I can probably come up with some reason as to why it can't continue. On the optimistic side it is possible that he may not be such a pain in the arse as he first appears: It could even work out well for both of us. After all we do urgently need somebody to assist; I know Gloria has managed pretty well up until now, but its quite ridiculous me expecting her to do everything. Like it or not, the business has grown rapidly; I have to recognise this and not fight against it. This is what I kept telling myself until

I had bored myself so much with the same persuasive argument that in the end I was beginning to believe it.

The following morning, a rather flushed looking Grimshaw arrived a few minutes after I'd opened the office. It was just after eight o'clock when he burst through the hardwood entrance doors wearing a navy pin striped suit with a black umbrella in one hand and an official looking brief case in the other.

"Good morning Clive", the wretched man he shouted enthusiastically; obviously full of joy with his new post.

"Good Morning," I replied: I simply couldn't deal with calling him 'Reginald'.

"How are you this morning?" He asked chirpily.

"Alright . . . I think," I replied. I'd always found it difficult to cope with these ebullient early morning exchanges. The natural cut and thrust of any witty repartee I might have attempted probably would, I thought, have been lost on Grimshaw anyway; Better to keep the whole thing fairly polite and formal.

"Can I get you a coffee?" I asked.

"That would be nice," he said, demonstrably relieved that I was attempting to be sociable.

"It'd only instant, there's no finesse here I'm afraid."

"No that's absolutely perfect; no sugar and just a little milk please," he said nervously.

"If you want to grab a seat...anywhere . . . there . . . just park yourself there, that's Gloria's desk; I'll sort the coffee out then we can go upstairs to a room you can use for the moment."

I made two mugs of coffee and suddenly realised how easy it would be to doctor his with a few drops of strychnine if I'd had any. 'No I must stop thinking like this', I thought: I must put the past behind me or this is going to become something of a nightmare.

I handed him the cracked coffee mug and instructed him to follow me. Upstairs; most of my personal possessions had

167

been cleared out of the one room I had been reduced to; but the floor was still scattered with old socks, shirts and various items of discarded clothing. There were a few old take away cartons festering in a black bin liner in one corner and numerous empty beer bottles and lager cans strewn over the floor.

"Sorry about this," I said, I haven't had time to organise anything properly."

I then moved around at considerable speed stuffing everything into the black bin liner whilst Grimshaw stood by looking not just embarrassed, but completely dumbfounded. I now realised then that we didn't have anywhere for him to sit. No desk, no chair, nothing. I suspected that by now he had come to the conclusion that this was some sort of strange game I had planned in order to seek my revenge.

"Look, I'm sorry," I said, "I need to get some more office furniture; I hadn't actually thought about it until now. Perhaps it might have been better if you'd given me a few days to get things organised."

"Oh I really am sorry," he said, "I didn't mean to rush you . . . it's just . . . I was . . ."

"No, no, it's not a problem," I said, realising my insensitivity and regretting not being a little more considerate and diplomatic.

"I know what we'll do," I said, "there's a second hand office furniture shop a few yards down the road: if you wait here; grab yourself another coffee; I'll pop down there and pick up another desk and a chair for you to sit on."

"Well let me come with you," he said. "After all you may need a hand to get the things back here."

This was indeed true: I hadn't thought about this. As the shop was only fifty yards or so away; he and I could carry the desk back; as I had done with all the other furniture.

When we arrived at the shop I couldn't help noticing that he seemed to be enjoying himself: the whole escapade was something quite new to him, something he'd never

168

experienced. What did trouble me though was the fact that he had seemed to set his sights on a large Victorian leather bound partners desk; a massive piece of furniture about six feet long and three feet wide. Although the top was badly stained, and the leather covering was ripped; he was convinced it was a bargain at sixty pounds. The chair he chose to accompany it was a massive leather swivel on an enormous chrome base. The leather had tears and rips in it but together the two items looked quite impressive. Poor old Grimshaw, I thought; he's still suffering from delusions of grandeur. After a little bargaining I managed to buy the two items for seventy pounds: far more than I had spent to date on any other office furniture, but if it made Grimshaw feel important again, I thought it would be money well spent. The next problem we had was trying to lift the desk. Although it was in three sections; the top, and the two pedestals: Grimshaw's face took on a frightening scarlet colour with tinges of blue around the cheek bones as we held the weight of it. This problem was quickly solved with a phone call to the office. Within a couple of minutes one of our vans had loaded all the items and was going to take them straight up to Grimshaw's new office.

It wasn't my imagination; he was really quite excited with his 'new' second hand office furniture. Obviously part of it was due to the fact that he'd now got something to do rather than sit in his roof staring at his train set and wondering what Hilda and her personal trainer were up to. My feelings towards him were distinctly dichotomised in that I felt sorry for him as you might any other human being that has had their whole world crumble in on top of them: and overwhelming feelings of contempt and hatred for the smug soft decades he'd spent as a pompous middle class bank manager. The only way I could manage these sentiments was to remain aloof and somewhat austere.

Back at the office, the 'new' desk looked very impressive. Grimshaw positioned himself behind it and surveyed his surroundings.

"Just the job," he declared. "Now let's get down to business."

Within an hour or so, he'd gathered up all the books, accounts, ledgers, and several mountains of paperwork; placed a pair of gold half moon glasses on the end of his crimson nose and started tapping away on a little adding machine that must have been tucked away in his brief case.

"Right, I'll leave you to it; if there's anything you need Gloria will know where it is."

"That's fine Clive," he said without looking up; clearly engrossed as he was in totting up something or other.

Chapter Twelve

It didn't take Grimshaw long to find his feet. After the first couple of weeks he'd prepared numerous charts, graphs, spread sheets, flow sheets, forecast summaries and God knows what else. The cash books, VAT accounts, wages and petty cash books had all been replaced with pristine examples of the correct type of ledger for each particular entry rather than our scabby assortment of books which Gloria and I thought would do. As the end of our 'extended' first year of trading was nearly upon us he'd written up a draft profit and loss account which according to him showed that we had made an enormous profit. Evidently we needed to lose some of this during the accounting year otherwise it would go in tax. Grimshaw suggested it would be a good time to give the office a serious makeover: spend some money on the basic office equipment that we had thus far done without. I was still stuck with the mind set that the business could still go under at any time and was probably being unnecessarily over cautious. According to Grimshaw this really was an irrelevance at this particular juncture: we had more than enough funds in reserve, and if we didn't reinvest some of it now in the business we would end up paying excessive amounts of tax. 'Better to have new office furniture and equipment, than just give it away to the tax man', he kept saying.

Despite my initial reluctance and caution; over the next couple of weeks the office was transformed from a dark makeshift third world refugee centre to an ultra modern swish centre for commerce. We had shining new hardwood desks, new computer systems, a complete new telephone system, banks of new filing cabinets, new carpeting throughout, together with large exotic looking plants artistically positioned with hidden spotlights focusing on them from different angles creating an atmosphere that reminded me of an upmarket American advertising agency. All the old furniture we had including Grimshaw's giant desk was removed by the second hand office equipment company where it came from, for which we were paid the grand sum of fifty pounds for the lot; the explanation being that there was no demand for it anymore. I just hoped now that the work would still continue to flow in. I hadn't placed any further adverts for quite a while: much to my amazement it didn't seem to be necessary. Whether it was word of mouth, or perhaps that Sprayum and Scarper were now out of the equation; I really had no idea but just hoped it would continue.

The initial four week trial period for Grimshaw had now elapsed and in accordance with our agreement I decided to speak to him about how he felt about things generally, and to see if he wanted to continue in his new role. I still found it hard . . .no . . .I think it would be more correct to say impossible . . .to call him 'Reginald'. On the few occasions when I found it necessary to address him I could only get the 'Reg' part of his name out. Occasionally I did call him 'Mr Grimshaw' but was told 'it's Reginald' again; not without some obvious annoyance on his part. Unfortunately his personal situation had deteriorated quite markedly since we had first spoken. His house was now in the process of being sold and the monies from the sale wouldn't cover all the debt that Hilda had run up in both their names. Even worse; Hilda had now issued divorce proceedings together with a claim for maintenance: not just a claim for maintenance, but for half of his pension from the bank.

172

"I'm done for, I'm done for," he kept wailing.

"What are you going to do?" I asked foolishly.

"I don't know; I just don't know," he groaned tearfully, "I will have to move out of our house soon: I was going to rent a flat, but now . . ."

"The court can't expect you to live on the street; surely?"

"I don't know, I just don't know," he kept repeating mournfully.

"Look Reginald," good God, I thought, I've actually managed to say it. "Why don't you go and see a solicitor. I'm sure things can't be as bad as they sound eh?"

"Yes, yes, I must: tomorrow I'll speak to Slimy and Rippumoff, yes I'll do that. I'm sorry to go on about it Clive; I'm sure you don't want to hear any more of my troubles."

"Right, now getting back to what I was saying; I just wanted to know if you were happy doing what you are doing here and if you wanted to continue . . ."

"Oh yes, most certainly yes, is the answer to that. Working here has taken my mind of things; I think it's actually kept me sane if you know what I mean. I just hope that you're happy with what I'm doing."

"Yes, yes, there's no problem as far as I am concerned; we did say we would talk about salary after the first four weeks, and I just thought I ought to mention it. I don't want you to think that I'm trying to take advantage of the situation. You should be paid a salary that the job is worth . . .that's all."

"Well, let me leave that up to you: whatever increase you decide to give me I will be happy with; after all I am fully aware that I'm in no position to make demands at the moment, so I really . . .I."

"Ok, ok, I was thinking of a twenty five per cent increase if that's alright, and as you now make up the wages and salaries, I'll leave you to adjust it accordingly."

"That's very good of you: very generous if I may say so; and I would just like to say thank you very much for everything."

As time went on I began to realise that my own position within the new company was, or had now become almost superfluous. Grimshaw was now firmly ensconced running the accounts and day to day financial matters; Gloria and the other girls were dealing with the general office administration, and the estimators I had employed were servicing the enquiries and booking in the work. In my efforts to delegate, I had virtually made myself redundant. I sat for many hours in my little cubicle of an office watching the frenetic activity going on all around me, of which I played no active part; I wondered sometimes what my function was in what had now evolved into a slick commercial enterprise that was wholly concerned with minimising costs, and maximising profits. The initial concept had now become a fading dream. I knew now, and had proven beyond any doubt, that my initial childish aspirations of setting up and running a moral and ethical business were naive into the bargain; particularly in this sort of business where there are really no common standards or controls and where exploitation is the name of the game. I had to accept that I now had little if any control in deciding what degree of work was actually necessary or being quoted for simply to increase the size of the job, or more often than that; just to get another job in: all of this was now an irrelevance. The hungry beast I had created required a certain amount of work every day and that was that. The estimators knew if they stopped feeding it, they themselves would suffer hunger. My role now was not exactly clear: a sort of office manager I suppose. The fact that it was my office and my business, didn't really make much difference. Having very few personal expenses; I now probably drew less out of the business than any of the other employees. Money wasn't, and had never been the motivation. I had abandoned my principles and was finding this the hardest part to accept. Ethical

174

Preservation was according to my accountant; was one of the biggest success stories he'd ever come across. To start a new business with very little capital during a recession, and one year later to have a turnover of nearly a million pounds was he said, quite remarkable. What he didn't know was that despite the name of the business; there was nothing ethical about it whatsoever. The start up capital came from tax evasion, drugs, and prostitution: and the bulk of the work that promoted our rapid expansion was acquired by undercutting Sprayum and Scarper and every other villain in the industry for work that probably wasn't necessary in the first place.

A few weeks after my discussion with Grimshaw; I noticed fairly late one evening whilst driving by the office that the lights were still on in his office. A few days later, I was walking by at about eleven o'clock at night; saw the lights on again, but this time there was Grimshaw standing by the window looking out at the traffic going by. Poor sod, I thought; he'd rather continue working in the evenings than go home to an empty house and contemplate his bleak future. It was somewhere around this time that Gloria had mentioned that one of the estimators upstairs must have been caught in a cloudburst on his way to work, as she'd found socks and pants draped over the radiator in the first floor bathroom. I'd also noticed a delicious smell of bacon when I arrived at the office a couple of times early in the morning. I didn't pay any further attention to it; I just assumed that one of the estimators had bought a bacon sandwich on his way into the office .The penny finally dropped when I considered that whatever time in the morning; no matter how early I arrived at the office, I could always hear somebody moving around above; the toilet cistern flushing, the bath running and so on: it was of course Grimshaw. He'd now completed the sale of his house and obviously had nowhere to go. The wretched man was now living in his office; using the kitchen and bathroom when everyone had gone home, or before they arrived for work in the morning. This was definitely the last straw; how dare he

175

do this without saying anything: even if it is supposed to be for just a few days. What would it be like if the rest of the employees all decided to do the same? Ok, I might be fairly easy going, but this is a downright abuse of my good nature. I decided I had to tackle him over this.

It was just after seven thirty the next morning; I unlocked the main office doors and walked straight upstairs: there tip toeing across the landing was a white blubbery body in a pair of Y fronts: the feet were sporting a pair of enormous furry slippers with grinning lion's heads covering the toes.

"What the bloody hell's going on," I shouted.
Grimshaw went ashen white and ran into the bathroom and locked the door. I banged on the door and shouted,"

"Grimshaw . . . I mean . . .Mr Grimshaw or Reg . . .Oh shit . . .look, you and I need to have a talk about what's going on here. I will be downstairs in my office; when you're dressed come straight down, alright?"
I heard a muffled 'yes' through the closed door, went downstairs and made some coffee. Ten minutes later Grimshaw appeared looking a little dishevelled, in a pinstriped suit with a face the colour of a tomato. He started talking before he even entered my office: obviously having rehearsed and practised whatever was about to follow.

"Look Clive, I can explain everything," he quivered.

"Go on then," I said.

"I had to move out of my house two weeks ago, you know . . . it's been sold; I did tell you that didn't I? Well the problem is that I can't afford to rent anywhere; even after selling my house I still have a considerable . . . well a mountain of Hilda's debts to pay off. If I didn't sleep here at night, I would literally be out on the street."

"Where do you actually sleep upstairs? On the floor?"

"Well, it's not far off it," Grimshaw's bloodshot eyes bulged as he despairingly shook his head from side to side. "I've got an old air mattress, it is a double one, but the bloody thing's got a couple of punctures in it: I blow it up just before

176

I settle down for the night . . . but a couple of hours later . . . the damn thing's flat again. It really is most annoying; I was going to go out today to try and find a repair kit for it, but I suppose there's no point now. Oh this really is a ghastly business: a ghastly wretched business; I'm so sorry for all the trouble I've caused you . . . I really . . . I really don't know what to say."

"Just a moment," let me think, I said to him, wondering what my next move should be. "Where's your furniture, you know, the stuff you had in your house?"

"It's all in storage; I didn't have time to sell it; things happened so quickly. I . . ." "Right, what I suggest is that you move some basic items; your bed and so on around to my house; you can stay there for a week or so until you get something sorted out. You can't possibly go on sleeping upstairs here: if other people starting doing the same, the whole building would end up like a cheap doss house."

"No, I understand," Grimshaw conceded. "That really is very kind of you. Are you sure I won't be too much trouble for you?"

No, I'm not sure at all; but if it's only for a week, or a couple of weeks; at least it will get you over this immediate crisis. What did you do with your train set by the way?
Grimshaw looked absolutely horrified. "It's not a train set: it's a model railway; a proper scale model; it's the only valuable thing I have left. It's in my office; it's all been carefully dismantled and packed away in boxes. I couldn't possibly allow that to go into storage; it might get damaged, stolen . . . anything could happen."

"I'd prefer you left it in your office, I certainly don't want it at my house; and Grim . . . sorry Reginald; I hope you understand this is to be a temporary arrangement. I don't care what you do with yourself in the evenings or weekends, but I value my privacy and I certainly don't want you sitting around with me. You can use the kitchen and bathroom at certain times which we will agree, and after that . . . whether

177

you decide to go out, or go back to your room, that's up to you. I am not trying to be unpleasant, but I think we should understand one another in order to avoid any unpleasantness."

"Yes yes, I understand perfectly: I promise not to be any trouble, and Clive; I really do appreciate this, what more can I say?"

"Nothing," I said curtly. "The sooner this difficult period is over for you, and you get yourself sorted out; the better it will be for both of us. Now here is a spare set of keys to my house; you *must* remember the address," I said rather unkindly, "I suggest you phone the storage company and get them to drop whatever it is you're going to need around to there and get them to pick you up from here first: you can then go along with them and make sure that they've brought everything you asked for: you can also check that nothing is damaged. I'll go straight to the house now and clear out one of the bedrooms for you. I'll leave a note on the door so you'll know which room it is; ok?"

"Yes, of course, and thank you so much for this," he said pathetically.

That evening I had gone straight from work to meet a girlfriend: we grabbed something to eat and went on to a classical concert. For the past year or so my social life had been non existent . . . too much worry, stress, and an almost obsessive concentration in trying to establish some security and stability. When I arrived home at just after midnight, I'd completely forgotten that I now had a house guest. The first reminder was in the guise of a magnified pair of false teeth in a glass of water that were sitting on the bathroom window cill. On the radiator there were some enormous frayed Y fronts and two pairs of holey woollen socks. I stared at the teeth in horror which then seemed to be grinning back at me. 'Good God', I thought, what have I done? Is this an oversight? Or does the wretched Grimshaw think that I'm going to put up with this? Perhaps Hilda wasn't quite as unhinged as he'd said. Perhaps she'd simply had enough of

178

his voluminous pants hanging around everywhere, and the teeth . . . the false teeth strategically placed somewhere to greet her every morning; and the train set . . .the bloody train set. Maybe she was just cracking under the strain and found that retail therapy was just about keeping her on the straight and narrow. The kitchen downstairs contained further unwelcome surprises: the remnants of what must have been a massive fry up were everywhere. The kitchen was still full of blue smoke, a frying pan containing a blackened congealed mess with what appeared to be two sausages encased in it was left on one of the gas rings; opened tins of tomatoes, beans and mushrooms were stacked on top of the rubbish bin, and just about every cooking implement and utensil I had was stacked up in the sink. The floor had become a skid pan from a packet of butter which being too close to the gas stove had melted and poured over the floor. On seeing this I decided there was only one course of action left to me now: I would have to kill him. After this outrage there could be no further room for discussion.

I left everything where it was, closed the kitchen door, went into the lounge and poured myself a large brandy. I needed to think this over I decided. After the second brandy I had calmed down a little. Going up to his room now at one o'clock in the morning, giving vent to my anger wasn't going to achieve anything. After all the poor chap was obviously going through a most dreadful time; possibly the worst time in his sad pathetic life. I had the unfair advantage: it would be cruel and obscene to make him feel any worse than he does anyway. Any further humiliation or stress might well result in him topping himself. I knew that somehow I would have to find that extra degree of compassion and diplomacy to explain the house rules to him a little more succinctly without threats or intimidation. This wasn't going to be easy; I wondered if I perhaps needed some form of anger management therapy as my blood pressure and anger began to manifest itself once again. Just the very thought of me having to deal with his basic lack of common decency in a polite and overly sensitive request that he might at least consider washing the bloody dishes, and cleaning up my kitchen after his midnight orgy.

I was woken every hour or so through most of the night by Grimshaw's revolting bodily noises. The snoring was at quite an astonishing pitch; even with his door and mine both closed. The only brief reprieve from this particular sound was the terrifying eructations from every orifice that seemed to rock the whole house. Obviously mammoth fry up's just before retiring were something he should avoid at all costs. I was now beginning to understand even more why Hilda found some solace in her personal trainer.

As it grew light I heard some coughing and rather unsavoury hawking sounds coming from the adjoining room: a shuffling sound on the landing carpet and then the toilet cistern flushing several times. This was followed by a lot of banging and crashing sounds from the kitchen below. Thank God, I thought; he's at least had the decency to go down and clear up the mess in the kitchen. Assuming it was now safe, I ran into the bathroom to take a quick shower. The first thing I noticed was that the teeth had been removed, so had the socks and pants from the radiator. I hope he's not sitting in the kitchen waiting for a nice friendly early morning chat, I thought. I got dressed, tried to convince myself that I didn't have a hangover and went down to the kitchen: but there he was sitting at the table holding a mug of coffee.

"Ah good morning Clive, how are you this morning?" he enquired fervently.

"Ok," I grunted.

"I hope I didn't wake you this morning, I got up early to do the washing up."

"I know," I said, "I would prefer you did it after you've cooked something and not leave it overnight if that's alright."

"Yes, I will of course, I'm extremely sorry if this has annoyed you," he said.

"It hasn't annoyed me it's just that . . ." Oh bollocks, I thought, I really can't stand this.

"I wondered if I might grab a lift to the office with you this morning if that's alright?" he asked.

"What's happened to your car? I assume you have a car?"

"Well yes, I did have one but I decided to sell it. I didn't use it very much; besides I need every penny I can get hold of at the moment. Once I've cleared all of Hilda's debts and found somewhere to live, then I might think about getting another one."

That's great I thought; absolutely great; not only have I landed myself with this pathetic flabby swine; he thinks we are going to drive off to work every morning together like two old chums.

"I'm afraid not," I said. "I'm not going straight to the office this morning; I have something else to do first."

"Oh not to worry," he said, "I expect the walk will do me good."

This arrangement clearly wasn't going to work. I had intended going straight to the office but couldn't stand his presumption that he could join me. Now I would have to drive off in the other direction and kill an hour somewhere before I could go to work. That in itself was annoying and inconvenient enough; but he would be bound to ask the same question again tomorrow, the day after, and every bloody day that he was here.

I drove around the corner; stopped the car, and started writing out a list of 'house rules'. I started off with the kitchen: times when he could use it; leaving it clean, washing any dishes and utensils and putting them away after use etc, etc. I then went on to the bathroom. I was becoming more and angry as I scribbled out the list with a pencil stub on the back of a parking ticket. 'Number six' on the list read as follows; 'false teeth or any other prosthetic devices or contraptions that may cause shock or offence must not be left on display at any time.' The next rule was to prohibit the flagrant display of his frayed old Y fronts in any of the public areas. However I tried to word this it sounded quite draconian and unreasonable. I wanted to include a section on requesting lifts to work which starting off as; 'it is strictly forbidden for any occupant of the aforementioned property to request, cajole, wheedle or otherwise demand 'lifts' to and from ones place of work, or anywhere else for that matter'. As the list went on I became incensed; I screwed it up and threw it out of the window. Sod it, I said to myself; try and be reasonable; the poor chap's going through a really bad patch; with any luck he'll be gone in a week or so.

At ten o'clock in the morning I had a doctor's appointment. The lump on my back had now grown into something the size of a tangerine and was hurting when I moved, or even when I didn't move for that matter: the doctor took one look at it and declared that we had to part company immediately . . . the lump that is . . . and myself. A quick phone call to the hospital was made telling them to expect me and the lump; and one hour later I was queuing up at the admissions desk clutching a plastic bag containing what I imagined people needed for a short stay in hospital; according to my doctor I would in the hospital for two or three days. I phoned Gloria; explained this, and insisted that no one should attempt to visit me: especially Grimshaw.

The ward I went into looked like a world war one field hospital during the battle of the Somme. I counted thirty old iron bedsteads a couple of feet apart, each one containing very ill looking people; many of them covered in bandages, plasters, slings; some on traction and others with support frames and cages around their heads and necks. Quite a few had drips and various strange looking machines wired to them with lights flashing and dials flickering giving the impression that they were about to blow up. Several other people were hobbling about on crutches with legs in plaster; one large fellow with red hair and a red beard who looked a bit like Rasputin, was using a walking frame for support whilst dragging a heavily bandaged foot across the tiled floor leaving a trail of putrid smelling grey sludge which was oozing out of the bandage. The stench inside this ward was quite indescribable. I later learnt that this patient had advanced gangrene and that his leg was subsequently amputated below the knee. Any courage I might have had evaporated instantly. I wasn't just slightly worried about being in hospital; I was completely and utterly terrified.

I was just about to make a run for it when an attractive young nurse came over and showed me to a vacant bed and started the admission procedure. A consultant would be along to see me later, and evidently I was on his list for surgery in the morning. Feeling extremely vulnerable I delayed getting undressed until I saw the fellow arrive with a flock of thirteen year old medical students. After the initial introductions and formalities they all inspected the lump on my back. The consultant pressed it, poked it, and even listened to it through a stethoscope. 'We'll soon get rid of that for you', he said confidently, and explained that I would be taken down to 'theatre' at ten the next morning after a little prick in the hand to make me 'sleepy'. Imagining he might have been some sort of sexual pervert, I was going to advise him that I wanted nothing to do with it, but thought better of it. I spent the night fully awake; rigid with fear listening to the most incredible din: coughing, groaning, wailing and the stench from patients with intestinal disorders using bedpans and commodes constantly throughout the night. When it got light some east European women appeared and started mopping the floors with a strong smelling disinfectant: at the same time the breakfast trolley was wheeled in. For people looking so ill, I was surprised at the amounts of the quite disgusting food they put away. A few of us including myself were not allowed to eat or drink anything: something I was extremely delighted about.

"You'll just feel a little scratch," were the last words I remembered before waking up and seeing Grimshaw holding a bag of grapes and staring down at me.

I couldn't immediately work out where I was and imagined this must be part of a bad dream.

"How are you feeling?" he enquired.

"Fine," I said what the hell are you doing here?"

"Oh I just wanted to make sure you were alright, and to see if you needed anything. Do they know what it was yet?"

"What it was? What are you talking about?"

"The lump: we are all hoping that it's nothing serious," he said.

"I'm fine; I'd be grateful though if you'd leave me alone. I did tell Gloria that I didn't want any visitors."

"Ok, alright, I'll just leave these with you," he said nervously placing the grapes on the bedside locker. "I'll drop back later on and give you a chance to rest."

"Please Mr Grimshaw: Reginald, I mean, just leave me alone. I'm fine; in a few hours I'll be out of here. I dislike hospitals intensely, but I dislike visitors even more; do you understand?"

After some nodding, grunting, and shuffling around from foot to foot, he slowly crept out.

Unbelievable, I thought, I can't seem to get away from this utterly wretched Grimshaw wherever I go. The worst thought I had to contend with now was that he'd be waiting for me when I got home.

In the afternoon, the consultant returned and advised me that my erstwhile lump had been sent off to the histology lab and that there was nothing to worry about 'We'd like you to stay here tonight, and all being well you can go home tomorrow morning', he said.

At six o'clock the east European cleaners arrived with their mops and their buckets and proceeded to swab the floors over with the pungent disinfectant. A few minutes later the 'dinner trolley' was wheeled into the ward; the smell of which was quite revolting. Being told that I must eat something; I decided to sample the epicurean delights of cottage pie and broccoli. The moment I received this steaming foul smelling dish; the patient in the bed next to me decided to defecate. Not in a bed pan, but on a commode less than two feet away from me. The nurses did pull the flimsy curtains around his bed but it made little difference: my appetite vanished. I got up, walked about trying not to look at the other victims, and found the day room. An elderly alcoholic was perched on one of the shiny blue hospital chairs in there, looking around furtively and taking quick swigs from a quarter bottle of whisky. With a guilty expression on his face he passed the bottle across to me; I grabbed it and swallowed a few mouthfuls; the hit was instant . . . excellent medicine. After chatting with him having smoked two of his roll ups I ventured back to the ward. All I have to do now is survive one more night, I thought. The night for me, was definitely the worst part about being in hospital; it was quite impossible to get any sleep. The food came next on the list. Even if the food had of been edible, trying to eat in this sort of environment was impossible for anyone with finer sensibilities. I wondered how many people in hospitals die from sleep deprivation and malnutrition. At about three o'clock in the morning an old Jewish fellow in the bed opposite me started groaning eerily in the semi darkness. 'I'm dying, I'm dying', he called out; a nurse walked over to him told him not to be silly and to be quiet as he was waking the other patients. 'No, listen, I'm telling you I'm dying already, do something, help me," he said. The nurse tucked him in and told him to behave himself; 'try and go to sleep now, the doctor will be round to see you in the morning', she said.

The groaning continued for another ten minutes or so; which was followed by a blood curdling desperate shriek whereupon the top half of him slumped against the bedside locker knocking over his water jug and a small vase of daffodils. With amazing speed and professionalism a trolley

185

was wheeled in, the body was covered and wheeled out again; the bed was then stripped and remade in readiness for the next victim. I sat bolt upright and waited with my heart pounding wondering who would be next.

At eight o'clock the next morning I was allowed to go. I couldn't get out of there fast enough. When I got home the first thing I saw was a vase of flowers on the kitchen table with a 'get well card' propped up against them.

Good intentioned, as no doubt he was; this for me was the last straw. I'd made a big mistake in allowing Grimshaw to stay in my house and I knew that this happy relationship must end before I murdered him. I could just about cope with him at the office where he was out of my sight; but I certainly now couldn't stand his presence after work. He had to go and quickly.

I got the office around midday and after reassuring everyone that I was not on the way out; went up to see Grimshaw. I explained to him as tactfully and diplomatically as I could that although I might appear normal and well balanced; I was in fact extremely unstable and that if he didn't leave my house within the next forty eight hours I would very probably do him a serious injustice. As finances were a problem I suggested the company would pay the rent on a flat for him which lessened the blow a little for what was in effect a callous inhumane act on my part.

Three days later; Grimshaw found himself a flat that was large enough to accommodate not just him; but his train set as well. I still had visions of his baggy frayed Y fronts draped over the radiators in my house, and the false teeth grinning away on the bathroom window cill; but I imagined these memories would fade in time.

A few weeks later I received a letter from a man called Bill Crichton of Killemall requesting I contact him regarding a matter which he considered could be mutually beneficial. Being of a suspicious nature I suspected this was part of a plan to assassinate me before they suffered a similar fate to

Sprayum and Scarper. Despite a not inconsiderable degree of caution; I telephoned him and arranged to attend a meeting at their offices in London.

To my surprise they were interested it seemed in acquiring my business. The first set of accounts had now been filed at company's house; and having looked through them and considered the matter carefully they wanted to make me an offer. When they mentioned a sum equal to the first years turnover I was tempted to shriek with joy. After thinking it over which wasn't exactly difficult: I did the deal with them on the basis that they would retain Grimshaw's services for at least twelve months and continue paying the rent on his flat. I also insisted that Gloria and Ben would be allowed to stay on should they wish to do so. This wasn't an act of kindness on my part; more a case of easing my troubled conscience. Initially Bill Crichton was trying to include a clause in the contract that would compel me to stay on as a 'consultant' with the new company for a period of one year to ease the change over through. I resisted this vigorously; I wasn't enjoying my role in the business anyway, and the prospect of this was not at all appealing. I also now desperately wanted to get away from Grimshaw: the prospect of working closely with him for the next twelve months to ensure 'a smooth transition' which is exactly what was suggested, would have been a complete anathema to me. I had quite definitely had my fill of Grimshaw, woodworm, dry rot, rising damp, and probably most of all; of being a 'businessman'. I had already decided that I would start another small building company, and try and pick up the threads of what I used to do. The only difference this time would be the half a million or so I would have in the bank to fall back on if we were to go through a difficult period.

Harry was of course ecstatic; 'I've always had a bit of a nose for a winner' he said with a broad grin. 'If you want me to invest in another business you know where I am', he said.

Chapter Thirteen

I experienced a weird feeling of alienation and detachment a few days after the deal had been finalised. I should really have been overjoyed, but the feeling was more one of ambivalence. I missed Gloria's perky enthusiasm and the indefatigable support she had exuded throughout the 'birth' and finale for me of 'effycool preservation'. I was only too aware that without her the whole thing would have never happened. I'd given her and Ben ten thousand pounds each as a token of gratitude and hoped that they would both be happy working for the new company. One of the greatest joys for me now was knowing that I would never have to see or talk to 'Reginald' again. I certainly didn't wish him any harm, but I knew I'd made a big error of judgement in employing him and then of course I didn't have the heart to sack him.

I did feel a certain contrition knowing that the company I had established would continue to trade under the rather misleading name I had created and would now be just as unethical and ruthless as Sprayum and Scarper, if not worse. I did however find some appeasement for my troubled conscience in the knowledge that over twenty people were now employed who might otherwise be on the dole.

My next move now was to try to re-establish a small building firm again in an effort really to continue where I'd left off before Grimshaw's intervention eighteen months ago. I bought a new pick up truck and had 'Clive West Building Services' written on the sides of it which seemed like a reasonable start. I then contacted all the Architects I knew and explained that I was now back in business . . . or almost. Within a very short space of time I had secured two small building contracts. One was to carry our new fire regulations to an old Victorian rest home in Worthing; and the other was for a room in the roof conversion, and a small extension for a private client in Brighton.

Keith, who had been working for me in the previous company had now joined me and was as enthusiastic as I was to get started.

It was at the rest home that I met Julia. I hadn't anticipated that there would be so many sprightly old people rattling around there, nor that they would all be so fascinated in what we were doing. The work itself mainly consisted of replacing the existing internal doors with one hour fire resisting doors with self closing devices, and enclosing the existing staircase to provide an adequate level of fire resistance. In principle the job was very straight forward and should have taken us about three weeks from start to finish. What I hadn't anticipated were the Dickensian 'gongs' that were sounded every few hours just before breakfast, lunch, tea and supper. As soon as the gongs were struck, hoards of incredibly agile but nonetheless elderly people appeared from nowhere and moved at a phenomenal speed on walking frames, sticks and some of them on crutches towards the dining room. On the first floor there were ten rooms, four of which were shared. This meant that fourteen geriatrics on speed would all rush out of their rooms onto the staircase we were trying to work on in a desperate panic to get downstairs. I'm sure they couldn't have moved any faster if the property had been on fire. Any attempt to stop them or slow them down, would have; judging from the determined look on their faces; ended in physical violence. I suppose it was understandable; for most of them these gongs were the only thing they now had to look forward to.

Julia was in charge of striking the big engraved brass gong in the hallway. Every day, ten minutes before it was struck she would warn us that the stampede was about to begin. This allowed us the minimal time to remove any tools and materials off the staircase and then stand well clear. The ascent up the staircase after each meal break was much more sedate; it seemed to take about fifteen minutes for them having left the dining room to get safely back in their rooms again: or as was the case with many of them; to hover over us asking continual questions. We worked out that in total; nearly four hours a day were wasted because of all of this. One of the perks though of this particular job, were the hot buttered freshly made scones with fresh cream and jam that were served to us twice a day with a pot of good strong tea. The other perk of course was meeting Julia.

Julia was an extremely attractive woman of about thirty with a delightful smile and an outgoing friendly personality. I'd decided that I must get to know her a little more. Apart from the odd evening out now and then; I had been leading a fairly monastic existence for the past couple of years. My wife had run off with a rock musician, just before my previous building firm collapsed, and the last thing I wanted to consider was starting another relationship. For me I knew it would be a difficult thing to do anyway; but more so when your world is disintegrating before your eyes.

Despite the various hazards of the task we had to perform; the job soon came to an end. I continued though to see Julia. I learned that she was twenty nine, had been married for five years when her relationship hit the rocks a year ago. She had nowhere to live and found her job as a resident housekeeper at the rest home just over a year ago. As things developed and became more serious between us; it was decided that she would move in with me but still keep her job which she clearly enjoyed. I got the impression that Julia was reticent for some reason about talking about her past. All I knew was that she was an only child; and that her childhood had been fairly

190

boring and uneventful. Both her parents were still alive but she had stopped seeing them shortly after she'd got married. Evidently her parents weren't getting on at the time, and also didn't approve of the marriage. This led to repeated family arguments and ultimately, the rift between them.

I did tell her of course some things about my past, but neither of us wanted to dwell on what had gone on before: we both now had everything to look forward to and were excited at the prospect of being together and looking forward to what the future might hold for us. I explained briefly about what had transpired with me and my marriage; that I had just started another building firm after the last one I had was forced out of business by the recession. I chose not to mention my good fortune with The Ethical Preservation Company and just said that I had to spend just over a year working for another company. I didn't want to tell her that I'd just sold my business for a six figure sum; I felt that this could somehow ruin the balance of our relationship. I realised also that to most people it would seem absolutely crazy to do what I was now doing and not be sitting back enjoying the money.

I spent the next few days inspecting further potential jobs and preparing estimates. It was certainly satisfying to be doing something I enjoyed. Julia had a few days off and we spent the time buying things for the house which included new curtains to replace the tattered moth eaten old rags that had been hanging in the bedroom for the past twelve years. According to her I had been living like a tramp, which I suppose in some respects was probably not far from the truth. I did feel pangs of guilt though, when she insisted on paying for them; sooner or later I would have to come clean about my hidden wealth.

The following week Keith and I started our second job: a room in the roof conversion and a small single storey extension. The owner's wife, a squat dark faced woman with a moustache, was good hearted and pleasant enough but would chatter to us incessantly about her continuing health

191

problems. This included all the recent operations she had recently undergone including a hysterectomy. No gruesome details were spared. After the second day we were both bitterly regretting having taken the job on at all. This feeling was further reinforced when she would scream up to us whilst we were working on the roof that she'd made tea and a sandwich for us which was 'waiting in the kitchen'. On many occasions we would go down as instructed, knowing that this was all part of a cunning ruse to enable her to go into further explicit detail of some horrendous surgical procedure, that either she or the patient next to her had experienced. 'In the end' she would say with a sickly smile, 'they 'ad' it all removed'. The other extremely unpleasant aspect of this job was the revolting stench of the home made chicken soup she seemed to make every day in a giant saucepan that always seemed to be bubbling away on the gas stove. Next to this on the opposite ring would be another enormous saucepan containing her husband's old underpants which she used to boil up. 'I do like me white's nice and clean', she would say, as clouds of vile uric steam wafted around the kitchen enveloping the sandwiches she had prepared for us making them damp and soggy.

After the first week there both Keith and I feigned digestive illness's of one kind or another in an attempt to avoid these disagreeable little sojourns. Thankfully the pressure was taken off us to some extent when 'Mad Mick', the bricklayer arrived and started furiously digging the footings out for the extension behind the kitchen. 'Mad Mick' was extremely unstable and more than likely verging on complete madness. His relationships with women never lasted for more than three or four weeks at the most. He didn't have a fixed abode and tended to move in with whoever he struck up any sort of accord with: usually it was women who were down on their luck that he would pick up in pubs who for one reason or another naively thought it might be nice to have a man about the place. In between these times he would sleep in his Transit van outside whatever job he was working on. When the client went out, or if the property we were working on was unoccupied for a short while he would sneak in and use the washing facilities. On one particular job; a large country house we were working on a few years ago, he went off at lunch time to the village pub intending according to him, to have a couple of pints as he'd been rained off in the morning and was hoping the rain would ease off in the afternoon. The rain continued, and so did he . . .to drink until the pub closed. He then staggered back to the job and feeling tired and a bit the worse for wear climbed into the clients four poster to sleep it off. Mercifully the clients were staying away whilst the building work was in progress. We discovered him there the next morning snoring away like a train. He was undoubtedly an alcoholic and a very unpleasant drunk. He was nonetheless an excellent bricklayer.

This particular job seemed interminable. After eight weeks, just as we were about to leave; it was decided that 'as we were there' they might as well have the wall removed between the lounge and dining room, and a new patio laid outside the new kitchen extension. Luckily, we were able to leave this to 'Mad Mick' and got out as fast as we could. I did question this wisdom of this, imagining the sort of exploits he was capable of; but we agreed that neither of us could stand another day there.

The following day was a Saturday, Julia and I were at home having a leisurely breakfast; one of the rare occasions when we were not both rushing off to work or trying to organise something or other, when the telephone rang. Julia answered it, and a few minutes later walked into the kitchen looking quite pale and uneasy.

"There's a woman on the phone, she wants to speak to you."

"Which woman?"

193

"She said her name was Ruth Wiseman; she said it's urgent . . . in fact I think she's crying, she sounds a bit hysterical."

My first thought was why on earth she was phoning me. A few thoughts went through my mind as I walked towards the phone; perhaps Harry's finally been caught for tax evasion; maybe they've had a fire, a flood; God knows. I picked up the phone,

"Hello Mrs Wiseman, this is Clive, Clive West."

"He's gone," was all I heard her say which was followed by shrieks of desperate crying and wailing."

Assuming she was referring to Harry: I said "gone? Gone where?"

"He's left us," she managed to say.

"Left? Where's he gone? What's happened?"

"He's dead."

"Dead . . .How can he be dead?" I asked stupidly without thinking.

"It's the bloody Inland Revenue," she screamed amongst further wailing.

"What do you mean? What's happened? I said, trying to draw a picture in my mind as to what could possibly have happened.

"This morning we were just having breakfast when the postman arrived. There was a loud knock on the door; Harry answered it, and had to sign for something, a letter, a recorded delivery letter it was. He came back into the kitchen and opened it. It was a high court writ from the bloody tax man for three hundred thousand pounds. Harry went very red and almost blue in the face: shouted out 'Bastards' and then keeled over onto the kitchen floor."

"Oh dear, I'm sorry," I said instinctively. Is there anything I can do?"

"Yes, yes, I'm just hoping you'll help me, I really can't cope with organising anything. We've got two sons; one is in Australia, and the other one is in Canada. Even if they came

194

back, which I don't think either of them could at the moment, it still wouldn't be for a good few days, and I know that certain things have to be sorted out: the funeral arrangements and all that sort of thing. I just can't cope . . . I really can't. You and Harry were friends I think; weren't you?"

"Well, hmm, yes, yes of course." I said wondering if in truth I would have agreed with that statement.

"Where is he now?" I asked.

"The paramedics, the ambulance, they've taken him to the hospital," she said.

"Mrs Wiseman; try and stay calm, I'll call you back in ten minutes. I just need to have a word with Julia, my partner."

In truth I didn't have any idea of what I should say to her, or what I should do next. I wanted to speak to Julia. I was hoping that she had some experience of dealing with situations like this. Thankfully Julia was calm and took control of things. She phoned Mrs Wiseman back, offered the usual sympathy and condolences and arranged for us to call around to see her and prepare the ground for what was to follow. I did find it extremely distressing watching Mrs Wiseman wailing her heart out when Julia put her arms around her hugging her and trying to offer a few comforting words. I realised how different women are to men, or was it just that I was born with a detached, callous, almost psychopathic streak? What I found most disturbing was watching this elderly woman in such pain. The fact that Harry had snuffed it, for me was incidental. He'd lived a reasonably long life; had made loads of money, which really was what his life was about. He didn't exactly live in poverty. The chances are that the writ he received for three hundred thousand pounds was probably only a tenth of the amount that he really owed them, knowing him and how devious he was.

Eventually it was agreed that we would go and register the death, collect the death certificate, and arrange the funeral. Julia telephoned the rest home and explained what had happened, and was allowed to rearrange her shifts for Monday and Tuesday.

We were now in the first week of September; it was a beautiful late summers day; a magnificent clear blue cloudless sky with the temperature in the mid twenties with a very slight cool breeze. We were both feeling a little subdued after the mornings trauma. I suggested driving into the country, perhaps going for a late pub lunch and a walk afterwards. Julia was quite enthusiastic about this idea so we drove up to the Devils Dyke and watched the hang gliders for a while swooping like giant majestic birds across the valley. After what was presumptuously called 'a ploughman's' and a couple of pints of decent ale we set off on our trek. Neither of us had any idea where we were going or for that matter where we were. Three hours later we staggered back to the car, having been hopelessly lost with me wondering why the hell I suggested this walk in the first place.

Our first task on Monday morning was to call into Burnham and Berryman the local funeral directors. We were greeted sombrely by a middle aged woman that started bowing and nodding sympathetically before we'd had a chance to explain what we wanted.

"All our sympathies are with you at this sad time," she said without our having said a word."

"Thank you," Julia said softly.

"One of your parents is it?"

"No," Julia replied, "not exactly, it's for a friend of my partner's."

"Is the deceased a gentleman or a lady, may I ask?"

"He's a man," I said. "Or was a man, should I say." I replied realising now that this was virtually inferring that Harry might have changed sex during the transition between life and death.

"Ah yes," she said soothingly. "I'm so sorry," as she wiped an invisible tear from the corner of her eye.

In no time a very colourful brochure appeared in front of us showing photographs of highly polished solid hardwood coffins with ornate mouldings and solid brass handles, all of them lined with sumptuous mauve satin padding. Each one had an impressive name, and an even more impressive price. There were but to name but a few; The Ambassador, The Viscount, The Belmont, The Statesman . . . the list was endless.

"Christ, what do we do?" I asked Julia.

"Oh I think go for something in between, you know not too ostentatious."

"May I ask if the 'arrangements' are covered by insurance? Or is this something the family are going to deal with?" she asked not quite so sympathetically.

"It will be for the family, his wife, I guess." I replied.

"Well it's just you know a sign of respect . . . you know that sort of thing. We all want to feel that we've done everything we can for our loved ones at a time of great loss." she said with a sickly insincere and mournful tone.

"Yeah, I know what you mean," I said, "it's just that poor old Harry would turn in his grave if . . ." Julia gave me a sharp kick.

We then settled on a 'mid range' product which I could have made for a third of the price, but consoled myself with the knowledge that I wasn't paying for it. We arranged for some cars, flowers, and a few other items which Julia seemed au fait with, and left.

When the eulogy was read out at the church I was surprised to discover that Harry had been such a generous and selfless person. Evidently his whole life had been spent in the self-sacrificing care for others, never ending acts of philanthropy etc. This was obviously a different Harry to the one I had known.

The reception if that's what it's called after the funeral was a strange disconnected affair. Ruth Wiseman had employed some caterers at the Wiseman residence for what appeared to be a medieval banquet. There were three young serving wenches dressed in the shortest black mini skirts I have ever seen and a number of dodgy looking 'geezers' chatting them up or trying to. Ruth Wiseman seemed to have rapidly recovered her composure and wore an expensive looking evening dress which sparkled under the lights of the massive chandelier hanging over the dining table. The whole thing seemed quite incongruous and in many ways irreverent. We stayed for a short while and were mighty pleased to get out into the fresh air again.

As expected Julia bombarded me with questions as to what my relationship had been to Harry. How long had I known him? Why had his wife come to me for assistance when he died and not to one of the other people at the reception?

I had no reason to lie to her; and told her the whole story about Harry being an old client I used to work for occasionally. I told her about the money he'd lent me to start the business; how the business had expanded so quickly and then that I had sold it just before we'd met.

"It sounds like a big company you owned," she said.

"Well it was in a way. It sort of grew by itself really. I didn't plan it that way."

Julia seemed quite perplexed. I imagined she must have thought that I was trying to be modest.

"Did you get much for it when you sold it?" she asked.

"Yes I did. Just over a million, but I had to pay Harry twenty five per cent of that."

I could see instantly that she didn't believe me. I wanted to get this over with as quickly as possible.

"Sure, that's a nice little story, I bet you wish it was true," she said laughing.

"It's true . . . really. I was going to tell you before but I wanted us to get to know each other properly before money started contaminating everything. After paying Harry and some tax on the money, I was left with just over half a million."

"That doesn't make sense," she said. "I'm sure you got a good price for it and good luck to you; knowing you, you probably worked hard for it: but if you had half a million in the bank you surely wouldn't be running a small building business."

"That is precisely why I didn't mention it. I knew that's the first thing anyone would say. The whole point is I enjoy the work I do. I could of course invest it in the stock market and buy the financial times every day to watch the share prices rise and fall, or just invest it and live quite comfortably off the interest; but I would go mad doing that. I can do that when I'm seventy."

"Yes I see your point or at least I think I do. But why then do you still live in this house? Why don't you buy a bigger house, a new car, furniture and all the rest of the things that rich people have?"

"The answer is quite simple," I said, "I don't want to be like 'rich people'. That sort of life isn't for me, and never has been."

It did take a while but eventually Julia accepted that I wasn't completely unhinged. Provided I agreed that we could change the threadbare carpet in the lounge, she didn't seem too bothered. I offered to buy her a new car but this offer was rejected without any hesitation. She wouldn't be parted from 'Bertie' her treasured 1952 Morris Minor. I suggested that she gave up her job if she wanted to as there was really no need for her to work if she didn't want to. This suggestion caused her to look at me with utter amazement. 'Why would I want to do that?" she said, 'I love my job'.

A few weeks later the Grand Hotel in Brighton was bombed by the IRA. I couldn't help thinking about just how disappointed Cheatum would have been on finding out that the person he hated most in the world had escaped virtually unscathed.

It was around this time that I had returned from work to find Julia looking unusually distressed and agitated. She ran to the door and opened it as I was just putting my key in the lock.

"Clive, it's really strange; I've just had a telephone call from my father. I couldn't believe it was him. I haven't heard from him for . . .it must be getting on for seven years now. It was really weird hearing his voice again after all this time."

"Well yes of course it must have been," I said. "How did he know where you were?"

"That's exactly what I wondered, but apparently he phoned my ex husband David: you know; I told you we still keep in touch, and David told him that I was now living with someone and gave him our number."

"Right I see: but why has he decided to contact you now after all this time?"

"Well, that's exactly the first thing I thought, but he was saying that he'd just come out of hospital after what sounded like a pretty horrendous stomach operation and was finding it difficult to manage on his own at the moment. He sounded a bit desperate on the phone, so I told him to put a few things in a case, jump in a taxi and come round. Oh Clive, I'm sorry I know I should have asked you first it was just such a shock. I really don't know how bad it is, but I really couldn't refuse to help."

"Don't worry that's fine. You don't need to be upset on my account; he's more than welcome to stay with us as long as he wants until he feels a bit better. What time is he going to arrive?"

"Well he said about an hour and that was about forty five minutes ago, so anytime now really."

"Ok, I'll just jump in the shower quickly and get some of this mud and brick dust off."

"Oh Clive, thank you," Julia said giving me a hug and a kiss, "thank you."

"It's ok, and don't worry, I'm sure everything will be fine."

Twenty minutes later I was just walking out of the bathroom and heard a knock on the front door. Julia rushed to open it: I heard her say 'Daddy it's wonderful to see you again', and there standing outside, much to my horror and disbelief; was . . . Grimshaw.